SAME TIME, NEXT YEAR

**Center Point
Large Print**

Also by Debbie Macomber
and available from Center Point Large Print:

Bride on the Loose
Cindy and the Prince
Shirley, Goodness and Mercy
Where Angels Go
Some Kind of Wonderful

The *Blossom Street* Series
The Shop on Blossom Street
A Good Yarn
Back on Blossom Street
Twenty Wishes
Summer on Blossom Street

**This Large Print Book carries the
Seal of Approval of N.A.V.H.**

SAME TIME, NEXT YEAR

Debbie Macomber

CENTER POINT PUBLISHING
THORNDIKE, MAINE

This Center Point Large Print edition
is published in the year 2010 by arrangement with
Harlequin Books S.A.

ISBN: 978-1-60285-661-5

Library of Congress Cataloging-in-Publication Data

Macomber, Debbie.
  Same time next year / Debbie Macomber. -- Large print ed.
    p. cm.
  ISBN 978-1-60285-661-5 (library binding : alk. paper)
  1. Large type books. I. Title.

PS3563.A2364S26 2010
813'.54--dc22

2009038303

To Beth Huizenga, my friend.
I admire your strength, your romantic heart and your love of life.

Prologue

James had been warned. Ryan Kilpatrick, a long-time friend and fellow attorney, had advised him to stay clear of the downtown area tonight. The crowd that gathered on Fremont Street between Main and Las Vegas Boulevard was said to be close to twenty thousand.

But James couldn't resist. Although he had a perfectly good view of the festivities from his hotel room window, he found the enthusiasm of the crowd contagious. For reasons he didn't care to examine, he wanted to be part of all this craziness.

The noise on the street was earsplitting. Everyone seemed to be shouting at once. The fireworks display wasn't scheduled to begin for another thirty minutes, and James couldn't see how there was room for a single other person.

A large number of law-enforcement officers roamed the area, confiscating beer bottles and handing out paper cups. A series of discordant blasts from two-foot-long horns made James cringe. Many of the participants wore decorative hats handed out by the casinos and blew paper noisemakers that uncurled with each whistle.

James remained on the outskirts of the throng,

silently enjoying himself despite the noise and confusion. If he were younger, he might have joined in the festivities.

Thirty-six wasn't old, he reminded himself, but he looked and felt closer to forty. Partners in prestigious law firms didn't wear dunce caps and blow noisemakers. He was too conservative—some might say stodgy—for such nonsense, but it was New Year's Eve and staying in his room alone held little appeal.

Impatient for the fireworks display, the crowd started chanting. James couldn't make out the words, but the message was easy enough to understand. It amused him that the New Year's celebration would be taking place three hours early in order to coordinate with the one in New York's Times Square. Apparently no one seemed to care about the time difference.

As if in response to the demand, a rocket shot into the air from the roof of the Plaza Hotel. The night sky brightened as a starburst exploded. The crowd cheered wildly.

Although he'd intended to stand on the sidelines, James found himself unwillingly thrust deeper and deeper into the crowd. Luckily he wasn't prone to claustrophobia. People crushed him from all sides. At another time, in another place, he might have objected, but the joy of the celebration overrode any real complaint.

It was then that he saw her.

She was struggling to move away from the crowd, with little success. James wasn't sure what had originally attracted his attention, but once he noticed her, he couldn't stop watching. Joyous shouts and cheers rose in the tightly packed crowd, but the young woman didn't share the excitement. She looked as if she'd rather be anywhere else in the world.

She was fragile, petite and delicate in build. He saw that she fought against the crowd but was trapped despite her best efforts.

James soon found himself gravitating in her direction. Within minutes she was pressed up against him, chin tucked into her neck as she tried to avoid eye contact.

"Excuse me," he said.

She glanced up at him and attempted a smile. "I was the one who bumped into you."

He was struck by how beautiful she was. Her soft brown hair curved gently at her shoulders, and he was sure he'd never seen eyes more dark or soulful. He was mesmerized by her eyes—and by the pain he read in their depths.

"Are you all right?" he felt obliged to ask.

She nodded and bit her lip. He realized how pale she was and wondered if she was about to faint.

"Let me help." He wasn't some knight who rescued damsels in distress. Life was filled with enough difficulties without taking on another person's troubles. Yet he couldn't resist helping her.

She answered him with a quick nod of her head.

"Let's get out of here," he suggested.

"I've been trying to do exactly that for the last twenty minutes." Her voice was tight.

James wasn't sure he could do any better, but he planned to try. Taking her by the hand, he slipped around a couple kissing passionately, then past a group of teens with dueling horns, the discordant sound piercing the night. Others appeared more concerned with catching the ashes raining down from the fireworks display than with where they stood.

Perhaps it was his age or the fact that he sounded authoritative, but James managed to maneuver them through the crush. Once they were off Fremont Street, the crowd thinned considerably.

James led her to a small park with a gazebo that afforded them some privacy. She sank onto the bench as if her legs had suddenly given out from under her. He saw that she was trembling and sat next to her, hoping his presence would offer her some solace.

The fireworks burst to life overhead.

"Thank you," she whispered. She stood, teetered, then abruptly sat back down.

"You want to talk about it?" he asked.

"Not really." Having said that, she promptly

burst into tears. Covering her face with both hands, she gently rocked back and forth.

Not knowing what to do, James put his arms around her and held her against him. She felt warm and soft in his embrace.

"I feel like such a fool," she said between sobs. "How could I have been so stupid?"

"We're often blind to what we don't want to see."

"Yes, but . . . Oh, I should've known. I should've guessed there was someone else. Everything makes sense now . . . I couldn't have been any blinder."

He shrugged, murmuring something noncommittal.

She straightened, and James gave her his pressed handkerchief. She unfolded it, wiped away the tears and then clutched it in both hands.

"I'm sorry," she choked out.

"Talking might help," he said.

She took several moments to mull this over. "I found him with another woman," she finally said. "He wanted me to come to Vegas with him after Christmas, and I couldn't get time off from work. So I said he should go and have fun with his friends. Then . . . then I was able to leave early this afternoon. I wanted to surprise him on New Year's Eve and I drove straight here. I surprised him, all right."

And got the shock of her life, too, James mused.

"They were in bed together." Her words were

barely audible, as if the pain was so intense she found it difficult to speak. "I ran away and he came after me and . . . and tried to explain. He's been seeing her for some time. . . . He didn't mean to fall in love with her, or so he claims." She laughed and hiccuped simultaneously.

"You were engaged?" he asked, noting the diamond on her left hand.

She nodded, and her gaze fell to her left hand. She suddenly jerked off the diamond ring and shoved it into her purse. "Brett seemed distant in the last few months, but we've both been busy with the holidays. I noticed he didn't seem too disappointed when I couldn't get time off from work. Now I know why."

It was preferable to learn about her fiancé's roving eye before she married him, but James didn't offer platitudes. He hadn't wanted to hear them himself.

"The problem is, I really love him." She shook almost uncontrollably. "I want to claw his eyes out, and yet I know I'll always love him."

"Are you hoping to patch things up?"

She raised her head. "No. It's over. I told him that and I meant it. I could never trust him again, but you know what?" She hesitated and drew in a deep breath. "I think he was grateful when I broke the engagement. He doesn't want me back—he wants *her.*" She stiffened, as if bracing herself against an attack.

"It hurts right now, but it'll get better in time," James said, squeezing her hand.

"No, it won't," she whispered. "It'll never get better. I know it won't."

James partially agreed with her. Part of him would always belong to Christy Manning. Even now, he had trouble remembering her married name. She wasn't Christy Manning anymore, but Christy Franklin, and her husband was the sheriff of Custer County, Montana.

"Yes, it will, but it'll take a year," James said briskly.

"Not with me. I'll never get over Brett."

"You believe that right now, because the pain's so bad you can't imagine it'll ever go away, but it does, I promise you."

Slowly she turned to study him. "You know? It sounds as if you're talking from experience."

He nodded. "Five years ago the woman I loved broke off our engagement." He laughed derisively. "You see, there was a small problem. She married someone else while she was engaged to me."

"That's terrible," she said with a sigh of righteous indignation. "What kind of woman would do that?"

"It's not as bad as it sounds. You see, her parents are good friends of mine, and I realize now they pressured Christy into accepting my engagement ring. She was fond of me and agreed because she wanted to make her family happy. I don't think she ever realized how much I loved her."

"Do you still love her?"

It might have been a kindness to lie, but James found he couldn't. "Yes, but not in the same way."

"Despite what I know, I can't picture myself not loving Brett." She straightened and wiped the tears from her cheeks. "I suppose I should introduce myself since I've cried all over your shoulder. I'm Summer Lawton. From Anaheim."

"James Wilkens. Seattle."

They exchanged brief handshakes. Summer lowered her gaze. "I wish I could believe you."

"Believe me?"

"That it'll take a year to get over Brett. It doesn't seem possible. We've been dating for nearly five years and got engaged six months ago. My whole life revolved around him."

At one time James's life had revolved around Christy.

"We were apart for less than a week," Summer continued, "and I was so lonely, I practically went through contortions to get to Vegas just so we could be together tonight."

"The first three months are the most difficult," he told her, remembering the weeks after the breakup with Christy. "Keep busy. The worst thing to do is stay at home and mope, although that's exactly what you'll want to do."

"You don't understand," she insisted. "I really love Brett."

"I really love Christy."

"It's different for a man," she said.

"Is it really?" he countered. "A year," he reiterated. "It'll take a year, but by then you'll have worked through the pain."

Her look revealed her doubt.

"You don't believe me?"

"I just don't think it's possible. Not for me. You see, I'm not the type who falls in love at the drop of a hat. I gave everything I had to Brett. It's like my whole world caved in and there's nothing left to live for."

"Shall we test my theory?" he asked.

"How?"

"Meet me back here on New Year's Eve, one year from tonight."

"Here? In this gazebo?"

"That's right," he said. "Right here."

"Same time, same place, next year."

"Same time, same place, next year," he echoed.

One

Summer picked up the mail on the way into her apartment and shuffled through the usual bills and sales flyers. The envelope was there, just as it had been on the first of the month for the past eleven months. A letter from James.

15

He couldn't possibly have any idea how much she looked forward to hearing from him. The first letter had come shortly after they'd met on New Year's Eve and had been little more than a polite inquiry. She hadn't written him back mainly because she was embarrassed about spilling her heart out to a complete stranger.

His second letter had arrived February first. He told her about the weeks immediately after his breakup with Christy, how the pain had intensified when he'd expected it to lessen. His honesty and generosity touched her heart. It seemed uncanny that her anguish mirrored his so completely. She wrote back then, just a short note to tell him how she was doing, to thank him for writing.

That was how it had started. James would write at the beginning of every month and she'd answer. Gradually their letters grew in length, but were never any more frequent. She liked the formality of exchanging letters, preferring that to the quick and casual convenience of e-mail.

In the year since Summer had met James Wilkens, she'd been tempted to phone him only once. That was the day Brett got married. Ironically, his wife wasn't the girl he'd brought to Las Vegas, but someone he'd met recently. Summer had felt wretched and holed herself up in her apartment with a quart of gourmet ice cream and three rented movies. She'd made it through the day with a little fudge swirl and a lot of grit.

Holding James's letter in her hand, Summer tore open the envelope and started reading on her way into the apartment.

"That's from your lawyer friend, isn't it?" Julie, her roommate, asked. Wearing shorts and a halter top, Julie wandered barefoot through the apartment, munching on a carrot.

Summer nodded, kicked off her shoes and lowered herself onto a padded wicker chair. Her eyes never wavered from the page.

"He wants to remind me of our agreement," Summer said, pleased he hadn't forgotten.

"Agreement?"

"To meet him in Vegas on New Year's Eve."

"Are you going?"

Summer had always planned to follow through on her promise, although she probably should've thought twice about meeting a stranger. But he wasn't *really* a stranger. She felt she knew James, was comfortable with him. He was a friend, that was all, someone who'd been there when she needed him.

"Are you going?" Julie repeated.

Summer looked up and nodded.

"What's James like?" Julie asked, sitting across from her. The two of them had been close ever since high school and both of them were in the production at Disneyland. Summer had been especially grateful for Julie's unwavering friendship in the past year.

"He's older," Summer said, chewing the corner of her mouth as she tried to recall everything she could about him. "I'd guess he's at least forty. Kind of a stuffed shirt, to tell you the truth. He's about six feet tall and he must work out or something because I remember being surprised by how strong he was."

"Is he handsome?"

Summer had to smile. "You know, I don't actually remember."

"You don't *remember?*" Julie was incredulous. "I realize you were upset, but surely you noticed."

"He has very nice brown eyes and brown hair with some gray in it." She raised her hand to her own hair and wove a strand around her finger. "I'd say he's more distinguished-looking than handsome."

"Is there something romantic going on between the two of you?"

Summer did care for James, but not in the romantic sense. He'd helped her through the most difficult night of her life. Not only had she clung to him and cried on his shoulder, but he'd stayed with her until the early hours of the morning, listening to her pain, comforting and reassuring her.

"We have a lot in common," was all she'd say to Julie's question about a romance.

"I have a feeling about you and the mysterious James," Julie said, her forehead creased in a frown. "I think you're falling in love."

Love? Not Summer. She'd decided last New Year's Eve that she was finished with love. It sounded melodramatic and a bit ridiculous to be so confident that she'd never love again, but she'd come to that conclusion the minute she found Brett with his girlfriend. Her feelings hadn't changed in the past eleven months.

Although he'd never said as much, she was sure James felt the same way after losing Christy. It'd been six years, and from what she knew about him, there wasn't a woman in his life even now. There wouldn't be a man in hers, either.

This didn't mean that Summer never intended to date again. She'd started going out with other men almost immediately. Pride had prompted her actions in the beginning. Later, she wanted to be able to write James and tell him she was back in the swing of things. He'd applauded her efforts and recounted his own endeavors in that area after Christy had broken off the engagement. As she read his account of various disastrous dates, she'd laughed, truly laughed, for the first time in months.

"You're going to meet James on New Year's Eve, and everything will change," Julie said with a knowing smile.

"What do you mean, everything will change?"

"You won't see him as just a friend anymore," Julie predicted. "You might be surprised to discover there's more to him than you suspect."

"Julie, I told you he's got to be forty years old."

"You're sure of this?"

"No," she said reluctantly. "But . . . I don't know. I picture James sitting in front of a fireplace, smoking a pipe, with his faithful dog sprawled at his side."

"A basset hound, no doubt."

"No doubt," Summer agreed with a laugh. James was wonderful—no argument about that—but she could never see herself falling for him. Nor would he be interested in someone like her. The man was a distinguished attorney, while she starred in a musical version of *Beauty and the Beast* at Disneyland. Working in the theater wasn't an easy way to make a living, but Summer loved the challenge and the excitement.

"You might be surprised," Julie said again. The tone of her voice suggested that great things were going to happen for her friend this New Year's Eve.

New Year's Eve

Summer freely admitted she was nervous about the rendezvous with James. She got to the gazebo nearly fifteen minutes early and was astonished to find him already there. He was sitting on the bench, the one they'd shared a year earlier. In that moment Summer had a chance to study him with fresh eyes.

The first thing that struck her was that Julie was right.

He was nothing like she remembered. Dignified and proper to the very back of his teeth, but there was something compelling about him. She recalled how Julie had wanted to know if James was handsome. If Summer were to answer that question now, she'd give an unequivocal *yes*. But he wasn't handsome in a Hollywood sense. He certainly wasn't boyishly good-looking like Brett, with his sun-streaked blond hair. But James Wilkens was appealing in a way that spoke directly to her heart. She knew from his letters that this was a man of conscience, a man of integrity, a man of honor. All at once Summer felt as if the oxygen had flown from her lungs.

He saw her then and slowly stood. "Summer?" He sounded equally surprised. His eyes widened briefly.

"Hello, James. I'm early," she said, feeling guilty at being caught staring so blatantly. "I'm always early . . . it's a family trait."

"I am, too." He grinned. "Usually early, I mean."

Summer had been looking forward to this evening for weeks. There was so much she wanted to say, so much she had to tell him. All at once she couldn't think of a single thing. "The streets are crazy," she said in a hurried effort to make conversation. "I didn't want to risk being late."

"Me, neither," he said. "I hope you don't mind, but I made dinner reservations."

"Thank you." She stepped into the gazebo and sat down next to him.

"So," he said, as if he wasn't sure where to start. "How are you?"

Summer laughed lightly. "A lot better than I was last year at this time. I told you Brett got married, didn't I?"

"You wrote about it."

Summer rarely felt shy, but she did now. She owed James more than she could possibly repay. "Your letters were a godsend," she said, "especially during the first few months. I don't know what I would've done without you."

"You would've done just fine." How confident he sounded, as if there was never a doubt that she'd get over her fiancé's betrayal.

"The first of every month, I'd run to the mailbox. Your letters were regular as clockwork and I counted on them." It had become a ritual for her, an important part of her recovery.

"I enjoyed your letters, too," he said. Fireworks splashed across the night sky, momentarily diverting their attention. "Do you want to join in the festivities?" he asked.

Summer shook her head. "Do you mind?"

He smiled. "Actually I'm just as glad. The crowd got to be a bit much last year."

"I'm so glad you were there," Summer said fervently. "You were like a guardian angel. You helped me so much that night."

"You helped me, too."

"Me? How?" Summer could hardly believe that.

"It's true," James assured her. "Seeing your pain reminded me how far I'd come in the years since losing Christy."

"Was it worse knowing she'd married that sheriff?" Summer asked tentatively. For her, learning about Brett's wedding hurt the most. Friends, under the guise of being kind, were more than happy to relate the details and what they knew about his bride. Every piece of information had cut like a knife.

"Yes."

"Weren't you angry?" she asked. How anyone could treat James in such a shabby manner was beyond her. To be engaged to a man as wonderful as James and then to secretly marry someone else was the most underhanded thing Summer had ever heard of.

"I wasn't angry at first, so much as depressed," he said thoughtfully. "Anger came later. It's the reason I took up squash. I worked out my aggression on the court. It helped."

Summer figured that was a sport an attorney would enjoy.

"It must've been hard finding out Brett was married."

She lowered her gaze and nodded. "Other than

the first few weeks after he broke our engagement, the day of his wedding was the worst. It seemed so completely unfair that he should be happy while I was hurting so terribly. If it was ever in me to hate him, it would've been then."

"And now?"

"Now," she repeated. "I certainly don't hate Brett, but I don't love him like I did a year ago. He was a big part of my life, and for a long time my world felt empty without him."

"Does it feel empty now?"

"Not in the least. I'm happy, James, and I didn't believe that would ever be possible."

"Then I was right. It took you a year."

She laughed. "I'm over him and happy to be with you tonight."

"There isn't anyone I'd rather be with on New Year's Eve." He glanced at his watch and stood. "I hope you haven't eaten."

"I didn't. I only arrived a little over an hour ago, and I'm starved." She'd been anxious about their meeting, so her appetite had been nil all day. Her stomach wanted to make up for lost time now.

James led her into the Four Queens Hotel, weaving through the crowds gathered around slot machines and gaming tables. With several thousand people milling around outside, she'd assumed the casinos would be less crowded, but she was wrong.

James took her hand then, gripping it firmly in

his own. Summer was surprised by how good that felt. By the time they walked down the stairs to Hugo's Cellar, an elegant, romantically lit restaurant, Summer felt as if she'd survived a riot. So much for all the effort she'd taken with her appearance. She thought she was fortunate to be in one piece.

After a five-minute wait, they were escorted to a booth and presented with elaborate menus. Candles flickered gently, casting dancing shadows on the walls. The noise and bustle upstairs and on the street outside the casino were blessedly absent.

They dined in leisure, shared a bottle of white wine and a calorie-rich dessert. They had so much to talk about—books, movies, world events, their families and more. James asked about her job at Disneyland and seemed genuinely interested in her budding career as an actress.

When she learned he'd recently been appointed a superior court judge to the King County bench, she insisted on ordering champagne to celebrate.

"You should've told me sooner," she said. "It's such wonderful news—so well-deserved."

"It's just temporary," James explained, looking uncomfortable. "I've been appointed to serve out the term of Judge Killmar, who had to retire for medical reasons."

Summer wasn't sure he would've told her if she hadn't asked him about his own hopes and dreams. Only then did he mention it was one of his lifetime goals to serve as a superior court judge.

"You intend on running for the position yourself, don't you?"

"Yes," he said. "But the primary isn't until September, and the election's in November. There're no guarantees."

"You'll win," Summer told him with supreme confidence. Wagging her finger at him, she added, "And don't give me that look. I can't imagine anyone *not* voting for you."

James's eyes met hers. "You're good for my ego," he said. She thought she heard him mutter "too good" under his breath but decided to ignore that.

By the time they'd finished dinner, it was close to twelve. As they made their way out of the casino, someone handed Summer a foil crown and a noisemaker. She donned the hat and handed James the whistle.

The New Year was fast approaching, which meant that her night with James was nearly over. She didn't want it to be.

The crowds had thinned out considerably after the fireworks display. They were standing on the sidewalk outside the Golden Nugget casino when a cheer rose from inside.

"It must be midnight," James commented and ceremoniously blew the noisemaker. "Happy New

Year, Summer," he said in a voice so low it was almost a whisper.

"Happy New Year, James."

They stood facing each other, and then, as if this were the moment they'd anticipated all evening, slowly moved toward each other. Summer saw how James's eyes darkened as her own fluttered closed. She wanted this. Needed it.

She sighed audibly as his mouth settled over hers.

Two

Summer was no novice when it came to kissing, but James left her breathless and clinging to him for support. She hadn't expected anything like this. She'd expected them to lightly brush lips and then laugh and wish each other a happy New Year.

It hadn't happened like that.

The instant James's mouth was on hers, she'd gone languid. She was immobile, her arms locked around his neck and her body pressed intimately to his, her lips seeking more.

Summer would've liked James to kiss her again. And again. She didn't want it to end. But she didn't know how to ask him to continue.

Slowly, with what she thought might be reluctance, he released her. She stood there looking at him, arms dangling stiffly at her sides while her face reddened with embarrassment. She considered telling him she wasn't usually this blatant.

"Happy New Year," James said. He didn't sound like himself at all. He cleared his throat and swallowed visibly.

"Happy New Year," she whispered, and stepped away from him.

James reached for her hand and held it in his own. Summer was grateful for his touch. They started walking, with no destination in mind, or none that Summer was aware of. She looked at James, wondering if he felt as confused and uncertain as she did. Apparently he did, because he grew quiet and introspective.

"I believe I'll call it a night," he announced unexpectedly. He checked his watch and frowned. Summer suspected it had been a year since he'd last stayed up past midnight. He was so proper, so serious and sober. Yet she'd enjoyed every minute of her evening with him. They'd talked and laughed, or at least she'd laughed. James had smiled, and she had the impression he didn't do that often, either. Every time he'd grinned, Summer had felt rewarded.

Now she'd ruined everything. She couldn't bear to know what he thought of her. An apology, words of explanation, stumbled over themselves, but she couldn't make herself say them—because she *wasn't* sorry about their kiss. She'd savored it, relished it, and hoped he had, as well.

"I'll call it a night, too," Summer said. She

waited, hoping he'd suggest they meet the following day. He didn't.

By the time they returned to the Four Queens, where they were both booked for the week, Summer was miserable.

"James," she said as they walked across the lobby. Either she apologized now or regretted saying nothing. "I'm sorry. I . . . don't know what came over me. I don't generally . . . I can only guess what you must think of me and . . ."

"You?" He hesitated in front of the elevator. "I was wondering what you thought of *me*. I can only beg your indulgence."

The security guard asked to see their room keys before calling for the elevator. James easily produced his while Summer sifted through the contents of her oversize purse before finding hers.

The elevator arrived, and they both entered. There was no one else inside. Still, James didn't ask to see her again, and Summer's heart grew heavier as they ascended. Her room was on the tenth floor, and his was on the fifteenth.

The silence closed in on them. When the elevator stopped at her floor, the doors slid open, and James moved aside.

Summer glanced at him expectantly. Okay, so he didn't intend to see her again. It made sense, she supposed. A superior court judge wouldn't be interested in dating an actress.

"Good night," she said brightly as she walked out of the elevator.

"Good night, Summer," James said softly.

She hesitated, hoping he'd ask her at the last minute, but he didn't. Discouraged, Summer trudged to her room, unlocked the door and went in. She sat on the edge of her bed, trying to sort out her muddled thoughts.

When Summer had requested a week's vacation, she hadn't planned to spend every available second with James. She knew he'd taken the same length of time, and he'd probably been thinking the same thing.

She slipped off her shoes and wiggled her toes in the thick carpet. If it wasn't so late, she'd call Julie and tell her friend she was right. One evening with James, and she saw him in a completely different light. The moment she'd seen him in the gazebo that evening, she dismissed the father-figure image she'd had in her mind all these months. More than anything, that kiss convinced her James was more than a friend. What became of their relationship would depend on several factors, the most important of which was James himself.

The phone on the nightstand rang, and Summer groped for it. "Hello?"

"Summer, I'm sorry to bother you."

Her heart gave a sigh of relief. "Hello, James."

"I've got a rental car," he said. "I know it might

not be something you'd consider fun, but I thought I'd drive over to Hoover Dam in the morning. Would you care to join me?"

"Why wouldn't I consider that fun?" she asked.

"I'm sure there are friends here your own age you'd prefer to spend time with and—"

"Friends? I thought you were my friend."

"Yes, but I was thinking of friends closer to your own age."

His answer irritated her. "I'm not exactly sure what you're insinuating, but if it is what I think it is, you're wrong, James."

"Listen, Summer, all I want to know is if you'd like to join me in the morning."

That might have been his original question, but she wasn't finished with what she had to say. "I took a week's vacation, and I know you have several days. I don't expect you to entertain me, if that's what you're worried about, because I can find plenty to do on my own."

"I see."

"And yes, there are any number of people my age in Vegas. There would be in any city. If you want my company, fine, but if you'd rather not see me again, I can accept that, too." Not easily, but she'd do it and have a perfectly good week without him.

He was strangely silent.

"James? Are you still there?"

"Yes. Are you always this direct?"

"No, but I didn't want there to be any misunderstanding between us. I value your friendship, and I don't want it ruined because of something silly."

"Nor do I." A short pause followed. "Forgive me for being dense, but I'm not sure I understood your answer. Are you going to Hoover Dam with me or not?"

Summer had waited all evening for this kind of invitation, and now the words were almost anticlimactic. "Would you like me to come?"

"Attorneys do this all the time, you know," he said with a chuckle.

"Do what?"

"Answer a question with one of their own. Yes, Summer, I'd very much enjoy your company."

"Great. When do you want to leave in the morning?"

James told her, and they set a time to meet in the lobby. Summer replaced the receiver and lay back on the bed. She smiled to herself, eager for morning.

James hadn't thought of himself as all that old, since at thirty-seven he was the youngest superior court judge in Washington State. Being with Summer, however, made him feel downright ancient.

She was perfectly named. Being with her was like walking along Green Lake in the middle of August, when the air carried the scent of blooming

32

flowers and sunshine warmed the afternoon. She shone with a summery brightness that made him feel content. More than content. Happy.

James couldn't remember any time he'd smiled more than during their dinner together. She'd told him about playing her role at Disneyland. Her joy and enthusiasm for her job bubbled over like champagne. He could have listened to her all night.

She certainly hadn't done all the talking, however, and to his surprise he'd found himself telling her about the ins and outs of his own position with the court and the upcoming election, which was vital to his career.

His life was very different from hers. While Summer worked in the delightful world of fantasy, he struggled with the often cruel, unjust world of reality.

Naturally he couldn't give her any details about the cases he'd heard, but just talking about his short time on the bench had lifted his spirits considerably. It felt good to share his thoughts with her and he'd enjoyed her opinions and her sometimes unpredictable views.

Then they'd kissed. Talk about sexual chemistry! For the life of him, James couldn't explain what had happened when she'd slipped into his arms. He'd never intended the kiss to become that intense, but once he'd started, nothing could have stopped him.

He'd been afraid his reaction had shocked Summer, but apparently that wasn't the case. Later she'd apologized to him and James hadn't known what to say. She seemed to think she'd done something wrong. She hadn't. The truth was, she'd done everything right.

The next morning James sat down in the lobby to wait for Summer. He was excited about this outing. He'd decided earlier not to invite her, feeling it would be unfair to dominate her time. She was young and beautiful, and he doubted she wanted to spend her vacation with a staid older guy like him.

He'd gone to his hotel room and congratulated himself on not mentioning the trip to Hoover Dam. Ten minutes later he'd talked himself into calling her on the off chance she might be interested.

Well, she'd told him. A smile pulled at the edges of his mouth. Summer had seemed downright angry when he suggested she'd prefer to be with friends her own age.

James liked the idea of being her friend. The operative word being *friend.* He wasn't going to kiss her again—that was for sure.

First, he was afraid of a repeat performance of that kiss in the street. Secondly, he was way too old for her. He enjoyed her company tremendously, but then any man would. He wasn't going to ruin the bond they'd created; becoming romantically involved, if she even wanted to, would do exactly that.

Summer stepped off the elevator, and James watched as every eye in the place seemed to gravitate toward her. She was stunning. It wasn't the clothes she wore, although the pretty pink pants and matching sweater flattered her. It was Summer herself.

She searched the lobby until she saw him, and then she smiled. James felt as though the sun was beaming directly down on him.

He stood and waited for her to join him. "Did you have breakfast?" he asked.

She nodded. "Hours ago."

"Me, too."

"If you're ready, we can be on our way." All he had to do now was stop staring at her. . . .

A few minutes later, the valet took his ticket for his rental car, and they waited for him to drive the luxury sedan to the back of the hotel. When the car arrived, the young man opened the car door and helped Summer inside. James was almost jealous to have been denied the privilege.

They drove out of Las Vegas in companionable silence. James had studied the map so he knew which freeway to take.

"Do you ever think about her?" Summer asked.

James had no idea what she was talking about. "Who?"

She laughed. "That's answer enough. Christy. Your ex-fiancée."

"Ah yes, Christy." James mulled over Summer's question. "Sometimes. Generally when I'm feeling especially lonely or when I see a couple with kids. That's when I wonder what Christy's and my children would have looked like.

"Do you still think about Brett?" he asked.

She lifted one shoulder in a halfhearted shrug. "Sometimes. It's different with me, though."

"Different?"

"From what you told me about Christy, she went to Montana to help her sister and met someone there."

"She would've broken the engagement right away, but it seemed like a heartless thing to do over the phone." Despite everything James felt a need to defend her. "When she did get back, her mother had arranged for a huge engagement party and I was extremely busy with an important lawsuit. I never blamed Christy for not telling me about Cody right away. She had her reasons."

"*I* blame her," Summer said stiffly. "It was a rotten thing to do."

"You blame Brett, too, don't you?" This was what their conversation was really about, James suspected. Something had happened recently that had hurt her all over again.

"Right before I left," she said in a small voice,

"a friend called to tell me Brett and his wife are expecting a baby."

"A friend?" James wondered about that. There seemed to be a certain type of person who delighted in being the first to deliver bad news.

"I'm going to be twenty-eight next month," she told him.

He smiled. "From the way you said that, one would think you're ready to apply for your retirement benefits."

Summer smiled back. "I suppose I sound ridiculous."

"No, you sound hurt. It's only natural, but that pain will fade in time, as well, especially if you meet someone else and get involved in another relationship."

"You didn't."

James couldn't argue. "It wasn't because I'd dedicated myself to loving Christy for the rest of my life. To be fair, I'm not sure why I never got involved again. It's not like I made the decision not to."

"Do you date?"

"Occasionally." A few months ago, two women had let him know that they'd welcome his attentions. James was flattered and he did enjoy a night out now and then, but he could never seem to dredge up much enthusiasm for either woman.

"What about you?" he asked, then mentally kicked himself. The answer was obvious.

Someone like Summer had a long line of men waiting to ask her out.

"I don't date all that often," Summer surprised him by saying. "It's funny, when Brett and I first broke up I saw a different man every night. Within a month I was sick of it, sick of pretending I didn't care, sick of telling everyone about all the fun I was having."

"And now?"

"I haven't been out all month. December is crazy, anyway, with Christmas and family obligations and everything else. In November, I went to a dinner party with a member of the cast, but it was as friends, and it was more a favor to Steve than anything."

Silly as it seemed, James was offended that she didn't count their dinner the night before as a date. He certainly had. Their time together had been the highlight of the year for him.

"My parents want me married," she murmured thoughtfully. "They hinted at it over Christmas."

Now, that was something James could identify with. "My father's a longtime widower and I don't have any siblings. He's been hounding me for years to marry, but his real interest lies in grandchildren."

"I'm not willing to marry just anyone," she insisted.

"I feel the same way."

They glanced at each other and then immediately looked away. Silence again filled the car. James didn't know what Summer was thinking, but he knew where his thoughts were taking him and it spelled trouble.

As they neared the outskirts of Boulder City, James mentioned some of the local facts he'd read. "This is the only city in Nevada that doesn't allow gambling."

"Why?"

"It was built for the men who worked on the construction of the dam. I'd guess it has something to do with making sure the workers wouldn't squander their hard-earned cash on the gaming tables. If that happened, their families would see none of it."

"I wonder if it helped," Summer mused aloud.

The next hour and a half was spent driving over Hoover Dam. They didn't take the tour. The day was windy, and James was afraid Summer's sweater wouldn't be enough protection against the cold.

Once they were back on the Nevada side, they stopped long enough for pictures. James felt the wind as he took several scenic photos of the dam with the digital camera he'd bought last year.

Far more of his shots were aimed at Summer. She was a natural ham and struck a variety of poses for him. He wanted a keepsake of his time with her.

James asked another tourist to get a picture of

the two of them together. He placed his arm around her shoulder and smiled into the camera.

"Can you send them to me?" she asked, rubbing her arms in an effort to warm herself.

"Of course," James agreed, pleased that she'd asked.

He turned up the heater when they returned to the car. He noticed that Summer's eyes were drooping about ten miles outside Boulder City. He located a classical-music station on the radio, and the soft strains of Mozart lulled her to sleep.

She woke when they were on the Las Vegas freeway. Startled, she sat up and looked around. "Wow, I must be stimulating company," she said, and smiled.

"I'm accustomed to quiet. Don't worry about it."

"James," she began, then yawned, covering her mouth. "What do you think of women who ask men out on dates?"

"What do I think?" He repeated her question, never having given the subject much thought. "Well, it seems fine in theory but I can't really say since it's never happened to me."

"Do you view them as aggressive?"

"Not necessarily. I know women invite men out all the time these days."

She smiled, and her eyes fairly danced with excitement. "I'm glad to hear you say so, because I bought two tickets to a magic show. It's this evening at one of the other downtown hotels. I'd enjoy it very much if you went with me."

James had walked into that one with his eyes wide-open. "A magic show," he murmured with pleasure. He hadn't even dropped her off at the hotel yet and already he was looking for an excuse to see her again.

"It's the late show, as it happens, which doesn't start until eleven. You'll come with me, won't you?"

"Of course," he said. If he wasn't driving, James would have pumped his fist in the air.

Although she'd spent nearly the entire day with James, including lunch and a light dinner on the road, Summer counted the hours until they met for the magic show. She was dressing when the phone rang.

"Hello," she said, thinking it could only be James. Her heart began to beat faster.

"Summer, it's Julie."

"Julie!" Summer had tried to call her friend earlier that evening, but she hadn't answered either her cell or the apartment phone. "Happy New Year!"

"Same to you. How's it going with the distinguished attorney?"

Summer sank onto the edge of the bed. "Really well. By the way, he's a superior court judge now."

"Wow. That's great. So you're getting along

41

well," her friend echoed in knowing tones. "Do you still see him as a father figure?"

"No way," Summer said, and laughed. "There's less than ten years between us."

"So." Her friend's voice fell. "Tell me what's been happening."

"Well." Summer wasn't sure where to start, then decided to plunge right in. "He kissed me last night, and Julie, it was incredible. I don't ever remember feeling like this in my life."

"So you'd say there's electricity between you?"

That was putting it mildly. Hoover Dam should produce that much electricity. "You could put it that way."

"This is just great!"

"We went to see Hoover Dam this morning, and tonight we're going to a magic show."

"This sounds promising."

That was how it felt to Summer, as well. "James invited me to drive to Red Rock Canyon with him tomorrow to feed the burros."

"Are you?"

"Of course." It had never occurred to Summer to refuse. She didn't care if he asked her to study goat dung; she would gladly have gone along just to be with him.

"Julie . . ."

"Yeah?"

"Would you laugh at me if I told you I'm falling in love with this guy?"

"Nope. I've seen it coming for months. You pored over his letters, and for days after you got one, it was James this and James that. I'm not the least bit surprised. This guy must really be something."

Summer's heart sank as she confronted the facts. "He's a judge, Julie. A superior court judge. I'm an actress. We're too different. I live in Anaheim and he's in Seattle. Oh, it's fine here in Vegas, but once we leave, everything will go back to the way it was before."

"You don't want that?"

"No," Summer admitted after some hesitation.

"Then you need to ask yourself exactly what it is you *do* want," Julie said.

Her roommate's words rang in her mind all through the magician's performance. Summer sat beside James and was far more aware of him than the talented performer onstage. There was magic in the air, all right. It sizzled and sparked, but it didn't have a thing to do with what was happening onstage.

After the show, James escorted her to his car, which was parked in a lot outside the casino.

"You've been quiet this evening," James commented.

"I talked to my roommate earlier," she told him when he slid into the driver's seat.

"Does it have something to do with Brett?"

"No," she said, shaking her head for emphasis. When James inserted the key to start the car, she placed her hand on his forearm to stop him. "James," she said softly, "I know this is an unusual request, and I'm sorry if it embarrasses you, but would you mind kissing me again?"

He didn't look at her. "I don't think it's a good idea."

"Why not?"

"Considering what happened the first time, it seems unnecessarily risky."

"I see," she murmured, disappointed.

"Summer, listen," he said impatiently. "You're beautiful and very sweet, but I'm too old for you."

"If you're looking for an excuse, James, you're going to need something better than that." This was the second time he'd brought up their age difference, and it made her mad. "Forget I asked," she said heatedly. "It was a stupid idea."

"That's exactly what I said." He turned the ignition switch, and the engine fired to life.

"You're probably going to tell me you didn't feel anything. Go ahead and lie, but we both know that's exactly what it is—a lie."

James expelled a labored sigh. "I didn't say anything of the sort."

"Then you're afraid."

Summer noticed the way his hands tightened around the steering wheel.

"I prefer to think of myself as cautious."

"Naturally," she mumbled.

What surprised Summer was how much his rejection hurt. No doubt James viewed her as immature and naive. Pushy, as well. She was probably the first woman who'd ever asked him out and the only one who'd sought a kiss.

Shame burned in her cheeks. The sooner they were back at the hotel and she could escape, the better.

The engine revved, but they weren't going anywhere. In fact, James had pulled the car onto the side of the road.

"You might as well know," he muttered, turning off the car. "I've had one hell of a time keeping my hands off you as it is. It doesn't help that you're asking me to kiss you again."

Having said that, he drew her into his arms. His lips were hungry and hard, his kiss long and deep. He broke it off abruptly.

"There," he whispered. "Satisfied now?"

"No," she whispered back, and directed his mouth back to hers.

This time the kiss was slow and sweet. Her mouth nibbled his, and she was completely and utterly amazed by how good it was.

"Summer," he said, "we're going to have to stop."

"Why?" she asked, and her tongue outlined his lips.

James groaned, and she experienced an intense sense of power.

"I don't have a lot of control when it comes to you," he admitted.

"I don't mind."

"I wish you hadn't said that." He kissed her again, deeply, and when the kiss ended, she was clinging to James, mindless of anything but what was happening between them.

James rested his forehead against hers, his breathing uneven. After he'd regained some control, he locked his arms around her and drew her close. For the longest time all he did was hold her.

It felt like heaven to be in James's arms. Summer felt cherished, protected . . . *loved*.

"I was afraid of something like this," he said quietly.

"Something like what?"

He groaned. "Think about it, would you?"

"I *am* thinking about it. I don't understand the problem. I like it when you kiss me and touch me. I assumed you liked it, too."

"I do," he said. "That's the problem."

"If you say you're too old for me, I won't be held responsible for my actions."

He chuckled at that. "All right," he said, brushing the hair away from her face. "I'm not too old for you in years, but in attitude."

"Well, that's easy enough to change. We'll start first thing in the morning."

"Start what?" he asked, clearly confused.

She kissed him, letting her lips play over his. "You'll see."

Three

James was waiting in the lobby early the following morning. Summer's face broke into a disgruntled look when she saw him. Hands braced on her hips, shaking her head, she walked around him.

"What?" he asked, thinking he might have left part of his shirttail out.

"Where did you say we were going?" she asked.

"Red Rock Canyon."

"Do you always wear a shirt and tie to feed wild burros?"

James wore a shirt and tie to everything. "Yes," he answered.

"That's what I thought. Then I'd like to suggest we stop at a mall first."

"A mall? Whatever for?"

She looked at him as if she questioned his intelligence. "I'm taking you shopping," she announced. "If you have any objections, you'd better voice them now."

"Shopping," James repeated slowly. That was probably his least favorite thing to do. He avoided malls whenever possible. "But why?" he asked innocently. He wasn't giving in without a fight.

"Clothes," she informed him, then added in case he hadn't figured it out, "for you."

He frowned.

"You don't have to do this," Summer said. "I think you look wonderful in a suit and tie, but you'd be far more comfortable in jeans and a T-shirt."

So this was what she meant about altering his attitude. She hadn't mentioned that it involved torturing him by dragging him in and out of stores.

"James?" She gazed up at him with wide eyes. "Are we going to the mall or not?"

It was on the tip of his tongue to tell her he felt perfectly relaxed in what he was wearing. He would've said it, too, if she hadn't blinked just then and her long, silky lashes fanned her cheek. Without much effort this woman was going to wrap him around her little finger. James could see it coming, but he lacked the strength to offer even token resistance.

"How long will it take?" he asked, and glanced at his watch, trying to give the impression that the burros only made their appearance at certain times. They did, but not in the way he was hoping to imply. The minute they suspected visitors had something edible, they appeared.

"We won't be more than an hour," she promised. "Two at most."

He was being fed a line, and he knew it. They'd be lucky to make Red Rock Canyon before nightfall.

"All right," he said with a sigh, wondering how a mature, reasonable male would allow a woman he'd barely met to dictate his wardrobe.

A relationship between them was unrealistic for so many reasons. The age factor, for one. And then she lived and worked in southern California, while his life was in Seattle. He didn't know much about acting, but it seemed to him that if she was serious about her career, California was the place to be. Long-distance relationships rarely survived.

"You won't regret this," she said with a smile.

She was wrong. James already regretted it.

The only shopping mall he knew of in Vegas was the one located on the Strip between two of the largest casino hotels. He drove there and pulled into the underground parking.

When he turned off the ignition, Summer leaned over and kissed him.

"What was that for?" he asked, although he realized he should be counting his blessings instead of questioning them.

"To thank you for being such a good sport."

Little did she know.

To his surprise, Summer stuck to her word. It took less than two hours for her to locate everything she felt he needed. James followed her around like a dutiful child—and discovered he was actually enjoying himself. He let her choose for him, and she did well, generally picking styles he might have picked himself.

"I feel like I squeak when I walk," he said as he led the way back into the underground garage. Almost everything he had on was new. Right down to the running shoes and socks. He'd changed in a washroom at the mall.

"You look twenty years younger," Summer told him.

"In which case, you could be accused of cradle-robbing."

She laughed and slipped her arm through his. She pressed her head against his shoulder, and James derived a good deal of pleasure from having her so close. He was still trying to figure out how he was going to keep his hands off her.

"Sometimes it feels like I've known you forever," she whispered.

James felt the same way. It was as if she'd been part of his life for a very long time. "I have the feeling I'm going to have a huge long-distance phone bill once I get back to Seattle."

Summer closed her eyes and sighed deeply.

"What was that about?" He unlocked the car door and loaded the shopping bags into the backseat.

"I'm grateful, that's all," Summer told him.

"Grateful?" James asked, joining her inside the car.

She was quiet for a moment. "I don't respond to other men this way—the way I have with you. I can't give you a reason or a logical explanation. In the last year, since we've been writing, I've felt close to you. It's as if you know all there is to know about me. My secrets, my faults, every-thing.

"That night a year ago, when we met, was prob-ably the most devastating of my life. I don't know what I would've done if it hadn't been for you. Generally I'm the first person to dismiss this sort of thing, but I believe we were destined to meet."

James had wondered about that himself, although he'd always seen himself as a rational man. Of all the people in that massive New Year's crowd, they'd found each other. It had to mean *something*. He didn't doubt that fate, kismet or whatever you wanted to call it, had brought them together.

"I've never experienced the things I do when you kiss me," she confided.

She wasn't alone in that, either. He started the engine and pulled into the traffic that continuously flowed along the Strip. Concentrating on his driving rather than looking at Summer helped him restrain his emotions—and his impulses.

If they'd stayed in the parking garage much longer, James knew they'd have had a repeat per-formance of the night before.

Kissing her again had been a big mistake. He'd

spent half the night fighting off the image of her in bed with him. If he took any more cold showers, the hotel was going to complain about the amount of water he used.

Summer's voice was unsure when she spoke. "I thought that after last evening you wouldn't want to see me again."

James nearly drove the car off the road. "Why would you think that?"

She lowered her gaze to her hands, which were folded primly in her lap. "Well, I behaved so . . . brazenly."

"You?" She obviously didn't know how close he'd come to losing control. Superior court judges weren't supposed to lose control. James couldn't remember the last time something like this had happened. Probably because it never had . . .

"It's good to know I'm not in this alone. I don't think I could stand that."

"Trust me, I'm experiencing the same feelings you are," he told her in what had to be the understatement of the century.

"We'll both be going our separate ways in the next few days. Until just now, I didn't know if I'd ever hear from you again."

"We've been in touch all year—why would that end?" He didn't expect anything permanent to develop between them, though; that would be asking too much.

"We can take turns calling each other," she offered. "Maybe exchanging e-mails."

"All right," he agreed.

Summer was silent following that, and he was beginning to recognize quiet moments as a warning. "What's wrong?"

She glanced at him and smiled softly. "I was thinking it would be nice to see each other every once in a while. I hope I don't seem pushy."

Seeing her on a regular basis suited him just fine. They hadn't even gone their separate ways yet, and James was already starting to feel withdrawal symptoms.

"I could fly up and visit you one month, and you could fly down and visit me the next," she suggested, again sounding uncertain.

James's hands tightened around the steering wheel. He suspected that the more often he saw her, the harder it would be to let her go.

"You're not saying anything."

"I was thinking."

"What?"

The complete truth would have embarrassed them both. "I was reviewing my schedule." The primary wasn't until September, but Ralph Southworth, a businessman and longtime friend who'd agreed to head James's campaign, had made it clear long ago: From here on out, James's life wasn't his own. Every place he went, every civic event he attended, would be a campaign opportunity.

"And?"

"February might be difficult for me to get away." His workload had suffered because of this vacation, and another trip, however brief, so soon afterward could cause additional problems.

"That's okay, I can come to you. In fact, I've probably got enough frequent-flyer miles to make the trip free."

"Great. Then I'll try to come to Anaheim in March."

"Wonderful." She lit up like a sparkler on the Fourth of July. Then she hesitated and bit her lower lip. "April might be difficult. Disneyland stays open until midnight during spring break, and we add a second *Beauty and the Beast* show in the evenings. It's hard to get a free weekend then."

"We can work around it." He didn't want to mention that from June onward, his schedule would be impossible. There was no hope of visiting California, and even if she was able to come to Seattle, he couldn't guarantee he'd be able to spend any time with her.

"Yes, we can work around any obstacle," she agreed. But she didn't sound optimistic.

They were outside the city now, driving on a two-lane highway that led to Red Rock Canyon. "I'll be very involved in my campaign this summer." He didn't feel he could be less than honest.

"Summer's the busiest time of year for me, too,"

she said with an air of defeat. "But we can make this work, James, if we both want it badly enough."

It frightened him how much he wanted Summer, but he was a realist, so he pointed out the obvious. "Long-distance relationships hardly ever work."

"How do you know? You've had several and you speak from experience?"

James resisted the urge to laugh at her prim tone. If memory served him, his first-grade teacher, Mrs. Bondi, had used precisely that voice. Come to think of it, he'd been in love with her, too.

"You'd be shocked by how few relationships I've had," he confessed.

"Do we have a relationship?" Summer asked softly.

James certainly hoped so. "Yes," he answered. And then, because she seemed to need convincing, he pulled onto a dirt road, behind a ten-foot rock. A trail of red dust plumed behind them.

"Why are you stopping?" she asked.

James wore a wide grin and held out his arms. "It appears to me you need a little reminder of how involved we are." James knew he was asking for trouble. Trouble with a capital *T*. His resistance was about as weak as it could get.

"Oh, James."

"A few kisses is all, understand? I don't have much willpower when it comes to you."

"You don't?" The words were whispered.

"That's probably the most beautiful thing you've said to me."

"Has anyone ever told you that you talk too much?" James asked as his mouth swooped down on hers. He kissed her the way he'd been wanting to all morning. No, from the moment he'd watched her approach him in the gazebo.

He kissed her again and again, unable to get his fill. He demanded and she gave. Then she demanded and he gave. He moaned and she sighed. Then and there, James decided he'd do whatever he had to—move heaven and earth, take a red-eye flight—to be with her. He doubted once a month would be enough.

He plowed his hands into her hair and sifted the long strands through his fingers. With their mouths still joined, he lowered one hand to her throat. Her pulse beat savagely against his fingertips.

James had never thought of himself as a weak man. But with Summer he felt as hot and out of control as a seventeen-year-old in his dad's car.

Reluctantly he dragged his mouth from hers and trailed moist kisses along the side of her neck.

"James."

"Hmm?" He brought his mouth back to hers, kissing her slow and easy. Talking was the last thing on his mind.

She pulled slightly away. "James."

"Yes?" he asked, distracted.

"We seem—" she whispered breathlessly.

His lips returned to her face, lighting on her forehead, her nose, her chin.

"—to have company."

James went still. When he'd left the road, he'd made sure they were out of sight of other drivers. "Company?" he repeated. He could already imagine the headlines. King County Superior Court Judge Caught in Compromising Position in Las Vegas.

"They look hungry."

James's gaze followed Summer's. Burros, five of them, stood outside the car, studying them intently. They were waiting for a handout.

James grinned. At least the burros didn't carry a camera.

Summer smiled, too.

"I brought along a loaf of bread," he said, and reached into the seat behind him.

"Should we get out of the car?" she asked.

"I don't think that's a good idea." He'd read about the burros, but wasn't sure how tame they were. "Perhaps we should lower the window a bit and feed them that way."

Summer opened her window a couple of inches, far enough to ease a slice of bread out to the eager mouths. Just how eager was something they were to quickly learn.

"Oh!" Summer backed away from the window as a large tongue poked through the small opening.

Soon they were both laughing and handing out the bread as fast as they could. James was going to be sorry when it ran out. Summer certainly seemed to be enjoying herself, and so was he.

When the loaf was finished, they raised the windows. It took the burros a while to realize their food supply had come to an end.

When the burros finally left, James started the engine and pulled back onto the road. They drove for another hour, stopped and toured a visitors' center, taking in the beauty of the countryside.

James felt Summer staring at him as he drove back to the city.

"Now what?" he asked.

"I can't get over the change in you."

"You mean the clothes?"

"Yes. You look like a Jim instead of a James."

James grinned. "There's a difference?"

"Oh, yes, a big one."

"Which do you prefer?" he asked, studying her from the corner of his eye.

His question made her hesitate. "I'm not sure. I like the way Jim dresses, but I like the way James kisses."

"What about how Jim kisses?" The conversation was getting ridiculous.

"Too impatient, I think."

"Really?" He couldn't help feeling a bit miffed. "What's so wonderful about James?"

"His restraint. When James kisses me, it's as if

he's holding back part of himself. I have the feeling he's afraid to let go, and it drives me crazy. I want to discover what he's hiding from me. I know this probably sounds a little crazy, but I find James intriguing."

"And Jim?"

She giggled. "Don't tell him, but he's sexy as hell."

"Really?" James was beginning to feel downright cocky.

"He's got that devil-may-care attitude. I have a strong feeling we should be grateful to those burros, because there's no telling what could've happened between us in the canyon."

She was right about that.

"It's those shoes you made me buy," James told her. "The minute I put them on, I had this incredible urge to look for a basketball court and do slam dunks." James loved the sound of Summer's laugher. He'd never been one to tease and joke, but he reveled in her appreciation of his wit.

It was midafternoon when they arrived back at the hotel. After showing the security guard their keys, they stepped into the elevator.

"How about dinner?" he asked, hoping he sounded casual when in reality he felt anything but.

"Sure. What time?"

"Six," he said. Three hours, and he'd be more than ready to see her again. He wanted to suggest they do something until then, but didn't feel he should monopolize her time, although he'd pretty much succeeded in doing that anyway.

"Six o'clock. In the lobby?"

"The lobby," he agreed.

The elevator stopped at her floor, and Summer stared down at her room key. "I'll see you at six."

"Six." They sounded like a couple of parrots.

"Thanks for taking me this morning," she said, easing toward the door. "And for coming to the mall."

"Thank you." He bounced an imaginary basketball and pretended to make a hoop shot.

She smiled, and acting on pure instinct, James lowered his mouth to hers. The kiss was gentle, and when they broke apart, it was all James could do not to follow her to her room.

Summer sat on the end of her bed, trembling. She closed her eyes and tried to relive those last seconds with James and couldn't. Being in his arms was the only possible way to recapture the sensation she experienced each time she was with him.

Julie, her roommate, had known long before Summer had realized it herself. When James had asked her how often she dated, she'd invented an excuse to explain why her social life was nonexistent of late.

But it was really because of his letters.

Hearing from James had become an important part of her life. On the first day of every month she rushed to the mailbox, knowing there'd be a letter from him, each longer than the one before. She'd fallen in love with the man who'd written her those beautiful letters.

Unfortunately she hadn't realized it until she'd seen James. She was worried that she alone experienced all this feeling, all this awareness. But after he'd kissed her, she knew that couldn't be true. He felt it, too.

She smiled to herself, remembering how flustered he'd looked when she'd said they had an audience.

Summer smiled at the memory.

Lying down on the bed, she stared up at the ceiling and soon found herself giggling. She was in love with James. She didn't feel a second's doubt, not the slightest qualm or uncertainty. To think she'd actually believed she'd never love another man after Brett.

She might have drowned in a pool of self-pity if it hadn't been for James. She owed him so much.

As she considered their plans to continue seeing each other, she knew it would be difficult to maintain the relationship, especially since they lived such separate lives.

It would require effort and commitment on both their parts. Summer was willing. She could tell that James wasn't as convinced as she was that they could make this work, but she didn't harbor a single doubt.

Summer dressed carefully for her dinner date with James. She chose a simple sundress with a lacy shawl and pretty sandals.

He was waiting at the same place in the lobby, but he surprised her by not wearing a suit and tie. He'd worn one of the short-sleeved shirts they'd bought that day and a pair of khaki pants. For a moment she barely recognized him. He looked relaxed, as though he hadn't a care in the world.

"James," she whispered when she joined him.

"Jim," he corrected, and grinned. He placed his hand inside his pant pocket and struck a catalog pose.

Summer laughed delightedly.

"I hope you're hungry," James said. He tucked her hand in the crook of his arm and guided her toward the door.

"I'm starved."

"Great. We're about to indulge ourselves in a feast fit for the gods." When they reached the sidewalk of Glitter Gulch, the lights made it as bright as the noonday sun.

"I thought about the conversation we had this afternoon," he announced out of the blue.

"About keeping in touch?"

He nodded. "I'm not sure what we have, the two of us, but whatever it is, I don't want to lose it."

"I don't, either."

"I've only felt this strongly about one other woman in my life."

"I've only felt this way about one other man."

"If I was going to put a name on this . . . this thing between us . . ."

"Yes?" she asked when he hesitated. James was a thoughtful man. She didn't mean to rush him, but she wanted him to say what was already on the tip of *her* tongue. Consequently, she had no qualms about leaping in. "I love you, James Wilkens. I want to throw my arms in the air and sing."

He looked at her as if he were actually afraid she'd do exactly that. "What you feel is just gratitude."

"Gratitude," she repeated scornfully. "*Just* gratitude." She shook her head. "I'm capable of knowing my own mind, thank you kindly, and when I say I love you, I mean it."

"I see," James said, and his voice fell.

"You don't have to worry about telling me how you feel, either," she was quick to assure him. It wasn't necessary; his kiss told her everything she needed to know.

"But . . ."

She stopped in the middle of the crowded sidewalk and pressed her finger to his lips.

"I'm too old for you," he muttered.

She narrowed her eyes.

"But I'm crazy about you, Summer. Call me the biggest fool that ever lived, but it's true."

"Thank you very much."

James chuckled. "I haven't been doing a very good job of hiding how I feel. Maybe that's because I didn't expect to feel like *this*." He splayed his fingers through his hair. "In retrospect, I wonder what I did expect."

"I assumed we'd have dinner that first night and we'd talk about what we said in our letters, and then we'd more or less go our separate ways, me back to my life in California, you back to yours . . ."

"Really." He arched his eyebrows.

"I wanted Julie to fly in for the weekend, but she refused and I couldn't get her to give me a reason. I know now. She realized what I hadn't—that I'm in love with you. My feelings developed slowly over the past year, and Julie saw it happening." She inhaled a deep breath. "I don't want to lose you, James. We can make this work if we try."

"It's not going to be easy."

As his words faded an idea struck Summer. "Oh, my goodness."

James stopped abruptly. "What is it?"

"James." She clasped his arm as she stared up at him. With every passing second the idea gained momentum. "I just thought of something . . . wonderful," she said urgently.

"What is it?" His arm circled her waist.

"Oh, James. Kiss me, please, just kiss me."

"Kiss you *here?*" James asked, appalled.

"Never mind." She laughed and, throwing her arms around his neck, she stood on the tips of her toes and kissed him, a deep, lingering kiss that communicated her feelings to him—and his to her.

He stared down at her dumbstruck when she stepped away.

"James," she said breathlessly, "I think we should get married."

"Married." The word was barely audible.

"It makes sense, don't you agree? I know how I feel about you, and you've admitted your feelings for me. Here we are, both worried about the most ridiculous things, when we already have what's most important. Each other."

Still James didn't say anything. He looked around, and his expression seemed slightly desperate, but that could have been her imagination.

"I can guess what you're thinking," she said with a laugh, "but I've got an answer for every one of your arguments."

"We hardly know each other."

That was a pretty weak argument. "Is that so? You know me better than friends I've had all my life. You've seen me at my worst. You've listened to my pain and my frustrations. There isn't a thing I can't talk about with you."

He frowned, and Summer longed to smooth the lines from his brow and kiss away his doubts.

"Don't look so worried! Honestly, James, anyone would think you were in a state of shock."

"I am." This came through loud and clear.

"But why?" His hesitation took her by surprise. She knew the idea would take some getting used to on James's part. He didn't leap into projects and ideas the way she did. He was methodical and thoughtful and carefully weighed every decision.

"Perhaps I'm assuming something here that I shouldn't," she said slowly. "You don't want to marry me, do you, James?"

Four

Summer was mortified to the very marrow of her bones. Without even trying, she'd managed to make a complete fool of herself. James had never come right out and *said* he was in love with her. But with all their talk about how important they were to each other, she'd naturally assumed he cared as deeply for her as she did for him. She'd assumed he'd want to marry her.

"James, I'm sorry," she said in a weak voice. Past experience had taught her to right wrongs as quickly as possible.

"Summer . . ."

"Of course you don't want to marry me. I understand. Really, I do," she said and pretended to laugh, but it sounded more like a muffled sob. "Now I've embarrassed us both. I don't know why I say the ridiculous things I do." She tried to make light of it by gesturing with her hands. "I guess I should've warned you that I blurt out the most incredibly awkward stuff. Forget I said anything about marriage, please—otherwise it'll ruin our evening."

James was silent, which made everything ten times worse. She'd rather he ranted and raved than said nothing.

In an effort to fill the terrible silence, she started chattering, talking fast, jumping from one subject to another.

She commented on how busy the casinos were. She talked about the big-name stars performing in town. She mentioned a friend of a friend who'd won the California State lottery, and then brought up air pollution problems in Los Angeles.

"Summer, stop," James finally told her. "It's fine."

She snapped her mouth shut. How she was going to get through the evening without humiliating herself further, she didn't know.

Her stomach was in such a knot that by the time they reached the hotel where the restaurant was located, she felt sure she'd only be able to make a pretense of eating.

The hostess seated them, but Summer got up as soon as the hostess left them.

"If you'll excuse me," she said.

James looked up from his menu.

"I'll be right back." She was hoping that a few minutes alone in the ladies' room would help her regain her composure.

"Summer, wait," James said. "I don't want you to feel bad about this."

She nodded, determined to drop the subject entirely. "Did you notice they had lobster on the menu?" She didn't actually know if this was true or not.

"It's just that most men prefer to do the asking."

"Of course." And it went without saying that the very proper King County Superior Court Judge James Wilkens wouldn't want an empty-headed actress for a wife.

Summer asked a passing waiter directions for the ladies' room. As she walked across the restaurant, weaving around tables, she felt James's eyes following her.

Once inside the restroom, Summer sat on the pink velvet sofa and closed her eyes. After a number of deep, calming breaths, she waited for the acute embarrassment to pass.

It didn't.

Briefly she toyed with the idea of slipping away, but that would've been childish and unfair to James. His only crime had been his silence, and he'd already explained that was simply his way. Just like making a world-class fool of herself seemed to be hers.

Five minutes later she rejoined him.

He looked up, almost as if he was surprised to see her. "I wasn't sure you'd be back."

"I wouldn't be that rude. It isn't your fault I'm an idiot."

"Stop," he said sharply. "Don't say such things about yourself."

"I can't believe I thought you'd marry someone like me," she said, poking fun at herself. "The girl who always speaks before she thinks and leaps before she looks."

"As a matter of fact, I do plan to marry you." He announced this while scanning the menu, which he then set aside. He watched her as if he expected some kind of argument. Summer might have offered him one if her throat hadn't closed up, making talking impossible.

The menu slid from her fingers and fell onto the table. Nervously she groped for it.

"Have you decided?" James asked.

She stared at him blankly.

"What would you like to order for dinner?"

"Oh." She hadn't even glanced at the menu. Frazzled as she was, she chose the first thing she saw. "Chicken Dijon," she said.

"Not lobster? It isn't every day one becomes engaged. I think we should celebrate, don't you?"

Somehow she managed a nod.

The waiter came, and James ordered for them both, requesting lobster and champagne. Their server nodded approvingly and disappeared. A moment later he returned with a champagne bottle for James's inspection.

"We'll need to see about an engagement ring," James said as though they were discussing something as mundane as the weather. "I imagine Las Vegas has quite a few good jewelers."

The waiter opened the champagne bottle with a loud pop and poured a small amount into the fluted glass for James to sample. He tasted it and nodded. Soon both their glasses were filled.

Summer breathed easier once they were alone. "James," she whispered, leaning forward. "Are you sure you want to marry me?"

He leaned toward her, too, and a grin slowly formed. "Yes."

"All at once I'm not convinced I'm the right person for you."

"Shouldn't I be the one to decide that?"

"Yes, but . . . I'd hate to think we're reacting to circumstances that wouldn't repeat themselves in a hundred years."

"Then we'll have a long engagement. We'll both be positive before we take that final step."

"All right." Summer felt only mildly reassured.

"We'll continue to see each other on a regular basis," James told her.

"Yes . . . we'll need that." She didn't like the idea of being apart so much, but that couldn't be helped.

"I wouldn't want the engagement to be *too*

long," Summer said. "I dated Brett for five years, and we were unofficially and then officially engaged almost that whole time. We both know where that ended up."

"Do you wish you'd married him?"

"No," she answered emphatically. "I don't have a single regret. I know you'd never do the things Brett did."

James's eyes brightened with intensity. "It isn't in me to hurt you."

"And I'd never knowingly hurt you," she promised.

"In light of what happened between Christy and me, I'm not fond of long engagements, either."

"Do you regret not marrying her sooner? That way she would've gone to visit her sister as a married woman."

"I've thought about that," James said. "Christy would never have allowed anything to develop between her and Cody if we'd been married. Getting involved with him behind my back was almost more than she could bear."

"I see." Summer figured she could read the writing on the wall. "You wish you'd married her, don't you?"

"No."

His quick response surprised her. "Why not?"

"Christy Manning didn't love me as much as I loved her. I'm sure she would have done her best to be a good wife, and we probably would have grown close over the years, but she would've married me for the wrong reasons."

"The wrong reasons? What reasons?"

"She was trying to make her parents happy."

"Okay," Summer said slowly, still feeling her way carefully around the subject. "So neither of us wants a long engagement. How long is long? A year?"

"That's too long," James said with feeling.

"Six months?"

He hesitated. "That'll make it June."

"June's a nice month," Summer said without any real enthusiasm. "Will you want me to live with you in Seattle?"

"Yes. Is that going to be possible?"

"Of course." She nodded vigorously.

"What about your career?"

She lifted one shoulder. "To tell you the truth, I was getting a little tired of playing Belle anyway. From what I understand, theater in Seattle is thriving. There wouldn't be any problem with me being your wife and an actress, would there? You being a judge and all."

"None that I can think of."

"Good." Summer picked up her fork and ran her fingers along the smooth tines. "My current contract expires in April."

"April," James said. "Can you arrange a wedding on such short notice?"

"You bet I can," she said, grinning. "Oh, James, I can't believe this is happening."

"To be honest, neither can I," he admitted.

Summer had never seen him smile as brightly.

The waiter brought their dinner, and James looked at the man who was a complete stranger and said, "The young lady and I have just become engaged."

Their server smiled broadly. "Congratulations."

"Thank you."

Summer would have added her thanks, but James had shocked her speechless. He wasn't joking; he really meant to follow through with their wedding and he was excited about it. Excited enough to announce their plans to a stranger.

"This hotel has an excellent wedding chapel," the waiter continued. "I gather that more than one celebrity has been married in our chapel."

"Right here in the hotel?" James asked.

"Many of the larger hotels provide wedding services for their guests."

"Don't arrangements have to be made weeks in advance?"

"Not always," the waiter explained. "A lot of people don't decide which chapel to use until after they arrive. Apparently you can get married with a few hours' notice—if the chapel's available, of course."

"Of course," James murmured.

A look came over him, one she'd seen before.

73

"Our wedding will be in April," she said hastily.

"My very best to both of you." The waiter refilled their flutes with champagne.

"James," Summer said after the server had left their table, "is something wrong?"

"Nothing. What makes you ask?"

"You're wearing an odd look."

"What do you mean?"

"It's a look that says you're not sure you like what you're thinking. Or hearing or seeing. The same one you got when I said we had company in Red Rock Canyon the other day."

"In this case, it's what I'm thinking," he muttered.

"You want to call off the wedding?" She should've realized that when James said he wanted to marry her, it was too good to be true. This had to be the shortest engagement in history.

"I don't know where you get the idea that I'm looking for a way out when I'm thinking exactly the opposite. I can only assume impulsive thoughts must be transmitted from one brain to another." He drew in a deep breath and seemed to hold it for a long time. "Would you be willing to marry me now?"

"Now? You mean tomorrow?"

"Yes. Then we'll repeat the ceremony later with family and friends in April."

Speechlessness happened rarely with Summer, and yet James had managed to cause it twice in the same evening. Her mouth dropped open, but no words came out.

"Summer, have I utterly shocked you?"

"Yes," she admitted in a squeaky voice.

James grinned. "I'll admit this is the first impulsive thought I've entertained in years. If you can propose marriage at the drop of a hat, then I should be able to come up with something equally thrilling."

Summer knew she was going to cry now. She could feel the tears welling up in her eyes. She used her linen napkin to dab them away.

"Just remember when we tell the children about this night. You're the one who proposed to me."

"Children." Summer blew her nose. "Oh, James, I'm looking forward to being a mother."

"Then you agree to my plan?"

"Married twice?" Everything was going too fast for her. "I'd want Julie here as my maid of honor."

"Of course. We'll phone her as soon as we're finished dinner. I'll be happy to pay for her airfare."

The tears were back, filling her eyes. These were tears of happiness and relief; she loved him so much. "James, we're doing the right thing, aren't we?"

He didn't hesitate. "Yes. It's what we both want."

"You love me?" He'd never said the words.

His look softened. "Very much."

Her mind whirled with everything they'd need to do. "I'll have to tell my parents. You didn't intend to keep our marriage a secret from our families, did you?"

"No. I'll call my father, as well."

Already Summer could hear her mother's arguments "They're going to think we're crazy."

James grinned again. "Probably."

"What should we do first?" Summer asked as they left the restaurant after dinner.

"I suppose we should find an available wedding chapel."

"Shouldn't we contact our families before we do that?" This was the part Summer dreaded most, and she wanted it over with as quickly as possible.

"But if we have the chapel booked, we'll be able to tell them the time and place," James said.

"Oh, yes." Trust him to be so logical even when he was acting impulsive.

"The ring." James snapped his fingers. "I almost forgot."

"Don't look so concerned. We can pick something out later. A plain gold band is perfect for now. In April we can exchange those for a diamond if you want."

"I'd like you to have my mother's ring."

"I'd be honored to wear it," she said quietly.

He kissed her, and Summer blinked in surprise. It was the first time he'd ever initiated a kiss in public.

Since the waiter had mentioned the wedding chapel at this particular hotel, they tried there first. Summer hadn't expected it to be so easy, but booking their wedding took only a few minutes. The hotel would see to everything, from obtaining the license to the music and flowers. They'd be getting married at seven the next night.

"If I'd known it was this simple," James said as they walked back to the Four Queens, "I might have suggested it sooner."

Summer pressed her head against his shoulder. They stopped at a crosswalk and waited for the red light.

"I wish you'd kiss me again," she breathed close to his ear.

His gaze found her lips, and he cleared his throat. "I don't think that would be a good idea."

"I suppose you're right," she murmured, but disappointment underscored her words.

"You can call your family from my room."

"Okay," she said, but her mind wasn't on making the dreaded phone call as much as it was on being alone with James.

His thoughts must have been the same because their pace quickened as they hurried across the street and into the hotel.

The elevator ride seemed to take an eternity. As if James couldn't keep himself from touching her in some way, he reached out and brushed a stray curl from her cheek. His knuckle grazed her skin.

"I can't believe you're willing to marry me," he said.

"I feel like the luckiest woman alive."

"You?" He held his hand to his brow. "I want you so much I think I'm running a fever."

"I've got a fever, too. Oh, James, we're going to be so good for each other."

"Don't," he growled.

"Don't?"

"Don't look at me like that, Summer. I'm weak enough where you're concerned. Much more of this, and I'm going to make love to you right in this elevator."

Summer smiled and moved against the back wall. "You're so romantic, James—and I mean that."

"You're doing it again."

"Doing what?"

"Looking at me like you know exactly what I want. Your eyes are telling me you want it as much as I do."

The elevator eased to a stop, and the doors slid open. Summer's heart pounded fast as neither of them made the slightest effort to leave.

"We were going to call our families," she reminded him just as the doors started to close.

James swallowed hard. "Yes, of course."

With precise movements he led the way out of the elevator and down the hallway to his room.

She noticed that when he inserted the key his hand trembled slightly, and she loved him all the more for it.

"The phone's over by the—"

"Bed." She completed his sentence, and the word seemed to stick in her throat. She walked across the room and sat on the edge of the mattress, then picked up the phone to dial the familiar number.

It might've helped if she'd taken the time to figure out what to tell her parents. But she was afraid she'd lose her nerve.

She couldn't put into words what she felt for James. She'd never loved anyone this way, this much, and she believed he hadn't, either. They'd each been in love with someone else, and that other person had caused deep pain. This time was different.

She knew, even before they answered the phone, what her mother and father were going to say.

"James," she said, in a panic, banging down the telephone receiver and holding out her arms. "Please, could you kiss me first?"

She glanced over at the man she'd marry in less than twenty-four hours, and his face was a study in raw sexual need. He walked across the room. The bed dipped as his weight joined hers. With loving care he gathered her in his arms and claimed her mouth. The kiss was slow and sensual.

He broke away, and his breath was hard and labored. Eager for the taste of him, the touch and feel of him, she brushed her lips over the curve of his jaw, then brought her mouth back to his.

"Maybe you should call your father first," she whispered when she pulled away.

"All right," he agreed. Reluctantly he sat up and reached for the bedside phone. Summer knelt behind him, wrapping her arms around his waist and pressing her head against his shoulder.

"Dad, it's James," she heard him say.

"Fine . . . yes, Vegas is just fine." Summer could hear a voice on the other end of the line, but she couldn't make out what was being said.

"I'm calling to let you know I'm getting married."

The voice went silent.

"Dad? Are you still there?"

The faraway voice returned, this time speaking very fast.

"Dad . . . Dad . . . Dad." Each time James tried to cut in, he was prevented from saying anything.

In frustration, he held the phone away from his ear. "I think you'd better talk to him."

"Me?" Summer cried. "What do you want *me* to say?"

"Anything."

Summer took the receiver and covered it with her hand. "Just remember this when we talk to my parents."

"I will." He kissed her briefly.

"Mr. Wilkens," Summer said. It sounded as if the line had suddenly gone dead. "My name's Summer Lawton. James and I have known each other a year. I love him very, very much."

"If you've known my son for a year, how is it we've never met?"

"I live in California."

"California?"

"Anaheim. I'm an actress." She might as well give him all the bad news at once. She didn't dare look at James.

"An actress?"

"That's correct."

"You're sure you've got the right James Wilkens? My son's the superior court judge."

"Yes, I know. James and I are going to be married tomorrow evening at seven but we're planning a larger ceremony in April. We felt it was only right to tell you about our plans." Convinced she'd done a miserable job, Summer handed the telephone back to James.

Father and son talked a few moments more, and the conversation ended with James abruptly replacing the receiver. He looked at Summer, but she had the strangest feeling he wasn't seeing her.

"James?"

"He's decided to fly in for the ceremony."

"That's great. I'll look forward to meeting him."

"He's anxious to meet you, as well. He hasn't

set eyes on you and already he thinks you're the best thing that's ever happened to me."

Summer laughed and slipped her arms around James's neck. "He could be right."

James grinned up at her. "I know he is."

"I love you, James."

"I know. I love you, too. Now it's time to make that call."

Summer had been delaying the inevitable and knew it. She stared at the phone, expelled a heavy sigh and said, "All right, I'll call my parents. Be prepared, James. They're going to have a lot of questions."

"They couldn't be any worse than my father," he muttered.

"Wanna bet?" Summer punched out the number to the family home a second time and waited. It was the decent thing to do, call her family with the news of her marriage, but if they just happened to be away, out of town themselves, no one would blame her and James for going ahead with the ceremony.

Four rings. Summer was about to hang up.

"Hello," her mother answered cheerfully.

"Mom," Summer said. "It's me."

"I thought you were in Vegas this week with Julie."

"Julie couldn't come."

"You went alone?" Summer could hear the disapproval in her mother's voice.

"I met a friend here. That's the reason I'm calling."

"Your friend is the reason? What's the matter? You don't sound right. You're gambling and you've lost everything? Is that it?"

"Mom, it's nothing like that."

"I never did understand why you'd go back to Vegas after what happened there last year."

"Mom, can I explain?"

"All right, all right."

"I'm calling to tell you—"

"Don't beat around the bush. Just say it."

Summer rolled her eyes. She knew where her flair for drama had come from. "I'm getting married."

Her mother screamed, and the next thing Summer heard was the phone hitting the floor. Her father's voice could be heard in the background, followed by moaning and crying.

"What the hell's going on?" It was her father on the line.

"Hi, Dad," Summer said casually, as if nothing was out of the ordinary. "I called to tell you and Mom that I'm getting married tomorrow evening."

Summer's father said nothing for several seconds. "Do we know this young man?"

"No. But he's wonderful, Dad, really wonderful."

"Like Brett was wonderful?" her mother shouted into the extension.

"Helen, get off the phone. You're too emotional to talk any sense."

"Don't tell me what to do, Hank Lawton. This is our little girl who's marrying some stranger."

"His name's James Wilkens. He's from Seattle and, Daddy, I'm crazy about him."

"He's an actor, isn't he?" her mother demanded. "What did I tell you over and over again? Stay away from actors. But do you listen to me?"

"Mom, James is a judge."

Silence.

"Mom, Dad, did you hear me?"

"What kind of judge? Beauty pageants?" This came from her mother.

Summer almost groaned out loud. "No. Superior court. He was recently appointed to the bench and he'll run for election to his first full term this November."

"A judge, Hank," Helen said softly. "Abby's daughter married that attorney, and we never heard the end of it. Summer's got herself a judge."

"Would you like to talk to James?" Summer offered. It only seemed fair that he talk to her family, since he'd put her on the phone with his father.

"No," her father surprised her by saying. "When I talk to him, it'll be face-to-face. Pack our bags, Helen. We're headed for Vegas."

Five

"Summer," James said patiently when he saw her distress, "what did you expect your family to do?"

"I didn't think they'd insist on coming here," Summer answered. "I wanted it to be just you and me. We can involve our families later, in April. I felt obliged to let my parents know what we were doing—but I didn't expect anything like *this*."

"You don't want them to come?"

"No," she said quickly.

In some ways James could understand her regret. If truth be known, he would've preferred his father to stay in Seattle. As it was, James's time with Summer was already limited, and he didn't want to share with family the precious few days they had left.

"I'm afraid once you meet my mother, you'll change your mind about marrying me," she moaned.

"Honey, it isn't possible."

"My mother—she sometimes doesn't think before she speaks."

"I see." James felt he was being diplomatic by not mentioning that Summer possessed the same trait.

"My dad's really great . . . You'll like him, but probably not at first." She gazed at James with large, imploring eyes. "Oh, James, he's going to give you the third degree. I'll bet he's having a background check done on you this very minute."

"I don't have anything to hide."

"See, Dad's been working with the seamy side of life for so many years, he suspects everyone."

"He's a policeman?"

Summer nodded. "I don't think he trusts anyone."

"Summer, if twenty-odd years down the road our daughter phones to tell us she's marrying a man neither of us has ever met before, you can bet I'll have a background check done, too."

"You know what this means, don't you?" she said, biting her lip. "We aren't going to have much of a honeymoon."

James chuckled. "Wanna bet?"

Summer grinned.

If this woman's smile could be bottled, James thought, it would be the most potent aphrodisiac ever made. He couldn't look at Summer and not want to make love to her.

"What about Julie?" James said in an effort to get Summer's mind off her parents' imminent arrival.

"Oh—I nearly forgot my best friend." She reached for the phone and called Julie's cell.

Since there were a number of things to do before the actual ceremony, James walked over to the desk and sat down to write out a list, not wanting to forget anything.

He was only half listening to the conversation between Summer and her roommate when he heard Summer's soft gasp and the mention of Brett, the man she'd once loved. James's ears perked up, and his fingers tightened around the pen.

"What did you tell him?" Summer asked in low tones. This was followed by "Good. Then you're coming? Great. You might want to talk to my parents and see if you can fly in with them. I'm sure they'll be eager to pump you for whatever you can tell them about James." After a few words of farewell, Summer replaced the receiver.

James turned around in his chair, wondering if she'd volunteer the information about Brett.

"Julie's flying in, too. I suggested she catch the same flight as my parents." She seemed self-conscious all at once.

Her eyes avoided his.

"So I heard." James waited, not wanting to approach the subject of her ex-fiancé, hoping she'd save him the trouble.

After an awkward moment, she blurted out, "Julie . . . Julie said Brett phoned."

James relaxed, grateful she chose not to hide it from him. "Did she find out what he wanted?"

"No. She hung up on him before he got a chance to say."

James had the distinct feeling he was going to like Summer's roommate.

Summer's shoulders moved in an expressive sigh. "I don't think either of us is going to be nearly as happy once our families arrive."

"How bad can it be?" he asked. All he cared about, all that was important, was marrying the woman he loved.

"My mother's going to insist we follow tradition and not see each other all day."

James frowned. He wasn't keen on that idea.

"My dad will keep you occupied with a whole bunch of questions. If you've got the slightest blemish on your record, he'll find it."

"I don't. Trust me, sweetheart, my background's been scrutinized by the very best. Your father isn't going to find anything."

She laughed softly. "In which case, Dad will probably thank you repeatedly for taking me off his hands."

James laughed, too. "Never mind. By this time tomorrow, we'll be husband and wife."

Summer's parents arrived early the following morning with Julie in tow. By chance Summer met them in the lobby on her way down for breakfast. James had called her room an hour earlier, before she was dressed, to tell her he was headed for the coffee shop. Summer had been too nervous to eat then, but had developed a healthy appetite since. She'd need fortification in order to deal with her parents.

"Mom! Dad! Julie!"

They threw their arms around her as if the separation had been ten years instead of a few days.

"I called Adam and told him his little sister's getting married," were the first words out of her mother's mouth. "He's taking time off work and he and Denise are driving in for the wedding."

"Mom," Summer protested, "James and I are having another ceremony later."

"Fine," Helen Lawton said briskly, "Adam will be there, too. Now stop fussing. It isn't like I held a gun to his head and told him he had to come. Your brother *wants* to be here."

"Daddy." Summer hugged her father. Stepping back, she placed her hands on her hips. "James is squeaky-clean, right?"

"How'd you know I had him checked out?"

"You're my father, aren't you?" She slipped her arm around his waist.

"How'd you ever meet a man like this?" Hank Lawton wanted to know. "He's as good as gold."

"Yes, I know. He's wonderful."

James appeared then, coming from the direction of the coffee shop, a newspaper under his arm.

Summer made the introductions, and while Julie and her family checked in to their rooms, Summer and James reserved a table at the coffee shop. They sat next to each other, holding hands.

"Are you ready for all this?" he asked her.

"I don't know." She sighed. "My brother's

taking the day off and driving in for the ceremony. I thought we'd have a small, intimate wedding."

"It is small and intimate."

"My brother and his wife have three little kids, who'll probably cry through the entire ceremony."

"I don't mind if you don't," James said and gently squeezed her hand. "I suspect folks will talk about us the same way when we drag our children to family get-togethers."

"Our children," Summer repeated. She felt weak with pleasure at the thought of having a family with James. "I know I've said it before, but I'm looking forward to being a mother."

"Not nearly as much as I am to making you one," he said in a low voice. The teasing light left his eyes. "If you have no objections, I'd like a large family. Maybe four kids?"

"Four." She nodded. "I'd love to have four children. We're going to have a good life, James. I can feel it in my heart. We're going to be so happy."

"I feel that way, too. Being an only child, I was always drawn to large families. I suspect that's why I've been such good friends with the Mannings over the years."

"Christy's family?"

He nodded. "She's the youngest of five."

Her parents and Julie appeared just then, and ever the gentleman, James stood until the ladies were seated.

"I hope you don't mind if we steal Summer away from you for the day," Helen said even before she looked at the menu. "We have a million and one things to do before the wedding."

"We do?" Summer didn't know why she bothered to protest. She'd realized this would happen the moment her parents announced they were coming.

"First, we need to buy you a dress."

Silly as it seemed, Summer hadn't given much thought to her attire. A nice suit would do, she supposed, something flattering and stylish. The elaborate gown and veil could wait for the April ceremony.

"Then there's the matter of finding a preacher."

"The hotel provides a justice of the peace," James said.

"Do you object to a man of the cloth?" Hank asked sternly.

Summer wanted to leap to her feet and tell James this was a test, but she bit her tongue. Sooner or later her soon-to-be husband would have to sink or swim on his own with her family.

"Not at all. I'd prefer one myself."

Summer had to restrain herself from cheering. James had passed with flying colors.

"I've got the names of several ministers from our pastor in Anaheim." Her father patted his shirt pocket. "We'll leave the women to do their thing, and you and I can find us a proper preacher." His tone implied that his little girl wasn't being married by any justice of the peace.

"What about rings?" Helen asked.

"I thought I'd pick up a couple of plain gold bands for now," James explained. "I'd like Summer to wear my mother's diamond. She can choose the setting at a later date, and it'll be ready before the April ceremony."

Breakfast wasn't the ordeal Summer had expected. Julie sent her curious looks now and then, and Summer knew her friend was waiting for an opportune moment so they could talk.

"We'll meet again at what time?" Helen asked, glancing at her watch.

Summer's father studied his, while Summer and James gazed longingly at each other.

"Six," Helen suggested.

"That late?" Summer protested. They were being cheated out of an entire day. No one seemed to appreciate that her time with James was already limited.

"I'll see to everything," her mother assured everyone. "Hank, all you need to do is get James to the chapel on time."

"Don't worry about my not showing up," James said. "I'm deeply in love with your daughter."

Julie's elbow connected with Summer's ribs. "What did I tell you?" she whispered out of the corner of her mouth.

Julie had more than gloating on her mind, and so did Summer's mother. When they'd finished their coffee, Helen organized a shopping expedition. She made it clear that a suitable wedding dress wasn't the only thing on her list. If her daughter was about to marry a superior court judge, she'd go to him with a complete trousseau.

The minute Summer and Julie were alone in the store, her roommate grabbed Summer's arm. "I heard from Brett again," she whispered.

"Did he phone?"

"No. This time he stopped by the apartment, right before I left for the airport."

"No." Summer closed her eyes, not because she had any regrets or because she harbored any doubts about James.

It was as if Brett possessed some kind of radar that told him when he could cause her the most trouble.

"He's been asking about you. Apparently he talked with a couple of the cast members at Disneyland. Steve and Karen? Do those names sound familiar?"

"Yes." Summer clenched her fists. "I can't tell you how much this irritates me."

"You? The man's been making a pest of himself all week. According to Brett, you're pining away for him." Julie made a melodramatic gesture, bringing the back of one hand to her forehead.

"You've been unhappy ever since the two of you split up—he says."

"Oh, puhleese."

"That's what I told him."

"If I was pining for anyone," Summer said, "it was for James."

"Exactly. I told Brett that, too."

"Thanks."

"I explained, with a great deal of satisfaction, that you're involved with someone else now, and he should stay out of your life."

"Good grief, he's married and about to become a father. The man has no principles." The thought of Brett trying to reestablish their relationship while his wife was pregnant with their child made Summer sick to her stomach. "I'm glad to be rid of him."

"You couldn't be getting married at a more opportune time. I'm telling you, Summer, from the way Brett argued with me, your marriage is about the only thing that'll convince him it's over."

"You did tell him I'm getting married, didn't you?"

"Yes, but he wouldn't believe me. He accused me of fabricating the whole thing."

"Girls, girls." Helen returned with a salesclerk.

"I wonder how long it'll be before she considers us women?" Summer asked her friend under her breath.

By evening Summer felt more like a French poodle than a bride. She'd been shampooed, her nails polished, her hair curled, her body massaged and moisturized. She'd been in and out of more clothes than a New York fashion model. And she was exhausted.

The idea of a white suit for the wedding was one of the first ideas to go. Before Summer could argue, she was draped in satin and silk from head to toe.

"You look absolutely stunning," Helen said.

Summer wasn't sure she could trust her mother's assessment. Her eyes went to Julie.

"She's right."

"But what about April?"

"What about it?" Helen's hands flew into the air. "You'll wear the dress twice. Big deal. No one needs to know."

She tried another argument. "It's so much money."

"My baby girl only gets married once."

Well, no. She'd be getting married twice—to the same man, but still, there were going to be two ceremonies.

Julie arranged the veil and the long train for the photographer who was on his way, then handed Summer the intricate gardenia bouquet. "If you're going to throw that, just be sure and aim it my way."

Summer smiled. "You got it."

"Not yet, I haven't," Julie reminded her.

A knock sounded at the door, and Helen answered it. Summer didn't pay any attention, assuming it was the photographer her father had hired.

A few minutes later, Helen introduced the tall, balding man. "Summer, this is James's father, Walter. You should've told me he was a retired superior court judge himself."

Summer would have been happy to, had she known.

"My, oh, my," Walter said as he entered the room. He stood in front of Summer, hands on his hips, and he slowly shook his head. "And where did my son meet such a beauty?"

"Here in Vegas," Summer said. "A year ago."

"I was about to give up hope for that son of mine. It seemed to me he'd settled a little too comfortably into bachelorhood. This comes as a very pleasant surprise."

"I'm so glad you came to meet me and my family, especially on such short notice."

Walter withdrew a thick cigar from the inside of his suit pocket and examined the end of it. "Wouldn't have missed it for the world."

Walter sat down and made himself comfortable. After a moment he returned the cigar to his inside pocket. "I quit smoking five years ago and I still miss it. Every now and then I take one out and look at it, just for the thrill."

Summer could see she was going to like James's father.

"To be frank, I didn't think that boy of mine possessed this much common sense."

"He's a judge," Summer said, eager to defend her husband-to-be.

"When it comes to the law, James is one of the finest men on the bench. He seems to be worried about the November election, but as far as I can see, he won't have a problem. No, what I'm talking about is something else entirely."

Summer felt like sitting down, too. Both her mother and Julie had mysteriously disappeared, and since the photographer had yet to show up, she decided to relax.

"Have you seen James?" she asked, missing him dreadfully.

"Oh, yes."

"How is he?" She folded her hands, wondering what James was thinking and if he was sorry he'd gotten involved in all this. Everything had seemed so uncomplicated when they discussed it the night before.

"He's pacing in his room."

"Pacing," she repeated, certain this was a bad sign.

"It's just as well this wedding's going to happen less than an hour from now. I don't think your father and brother could keep James away from you much longer than that."

Summer smiled in relief.

"Never thought I'd see the day my boy would fall head over heels in love like this."

"But he was engaged before. I know about Christy Manning."

"Ah, yes, Christy. She's a dear girl, and James had strong feelings for her, but deep down I believe what he found so attractive about Christy was her family. There's quite a difference between the love James has for you and what he felt for Christy Manning. As you'll recall, he was content to stay engaged to Christy for a good long while. But you . . . He's marrying you so fast, my head's spinning. His, too, from the looks of him. You've thrown him for quite a loop."

"I love James, too," Summer said with feeling, "very much."

"Good. I hope the two of you will seriously consider making me a grandfather soon. I'm hoping for a grandchild or two to spoil."

"We'd like to have four."

"Four." Walter nodded, looking pleased. "But you're worried about something."

"Yes," she said softly, wondering how he knew. "My biggest fear is that I'm not the right kind of wife for James. I'm afraid I might inadvertently harm his career."

"What makes you think that?"

"I have this tendency to speak my mind."

"I find that refreshing."

"You will until I put my foot in my mouth and embarrass James. To give you an example . . ." She hesitated, not sure she should continue, then realized she couldn't very well stop now. "I'm the one who suggested we get married."

"Really?"

"It just . . . came out. It seemed like a brilliant idea at the time . . . you know how good things can sound until you've thought them through. Well, anyway, James stared at me like he'd swallowed his tongue."

Walter burst out laughing. "Forgive me, my dear. Continue, please."

"Naturally I felt like a fool. Mainly because James didn't say anything and didn't say anything and didn't say anything, and I was convinced I'd ruined everything."

"He said nothing, did he?"

"Well, he did mumble something about preferring to do the asking himself."

"And you clammed up."

"Oh, quite the opposite. I started talking at hurricane speed until he told me it was fine and I needn't worry. And then, after I'd fallen all over myself telling him how sorry I was, he said he thought it was a good idea. James came up with the idea of a ceremony now and then one in April."

"He did?" Clearly this was news to his father.

"Yes." Summer grinned sheepishly. "He said something about impulsive thoughts being contagious."

"There's more to the boy than I assumed."

There was another knock at the door, and the photographer let himself inside.

"I'd better get back to James," Walter said. "It's been a delight meeting you, Summer. I don't have a shred of doubt that you're the best thing to come into my son's life for a very long time. Make him happy, Summer, make him very happy."

"I intend to do my best."

"And while you're at it, teach him how to laugh."

Summer nodded. "I'll try." She had a sneaking suspicion they had plenty to teach one another.

James looked at his watch for the third time that minute. No one seemed to understand that he *needed* to see Summer. Needed to talk to her, find out about her day, tell her about his.

If he'd had even an inkling that their wedding was going to cause such a big commotion, he would never have agreed to contact their families.

James liked Summer's parents, but he'd prefer to spend his time with her. Alone.

"We can go into the chapel now," Hank Lawton said.

James was so grateful he felt like cheering. According to his calculations, the ceremony would take approximately twenty minutes, thirty at most. They'd sign the marriage certificate, and the rest of the night would be theirs. He couldn't tolerate any more of these separations, however brief. The next time Summer left his sight would be at the airport.

He saw her family in the small chapel, her brother's children wide-eyed and excited as the organ music rose triumphantly. He noticed that the wedding chapel was almost full and wondered for just a moment who the other guests were.

James went to stand in front with the minister, Reverend Floyd Wilson. James had rented the tuxedo because it seemed odd for the father of the bride to be wearing one and not the groom. Now, however, the shirt seemed too tight around the collar. He resisted the urge to insert his finger and give himself a little extra breathing space.

It was then that Summer appeared.

James felt as if someone had smashed him in the knees with a bat. Never in all his life had he seen anyone more beautiful. His heart beat so hard he thought it might pound straight through his chest.

Her dress was silk and lace with pearls, as traditional a wedding gown as any he'd seen. One would think Summer was a debutante and this a society wedding.

When she joined him at the altar and placed her arm in his, James felt this was the proudest moment of his life. He knew they'd repeat the ceremony in a few months, but nothing would match the blend of humility and pride he experienced right then.

Her brother, Adam, was kind enough to serve as his best man, while Julie, of course, was the maid of honor.

The ceremony itself was a blur. James's full concentration was on the woman at his side. He knew she was feeling the same emotions he was when she began to repeat her vows.

Summer's voice shook slightly, and she sounded close to tears. His arm tightened around hers as the minister said, "I now pronounce you husband and wife. You may kiss your bride."

James didn't need to hear that twice. Carefully he gathered Summer close, sighing when their lips met in the tenderest, sweetest kiss of his life.

She clung to him. "Oh, James, how soon can we get rid of everyone?"

He'd entertained that very question from the moment Summer's mother had taken her away that morning.

"Soon," he promised. Heaven only knew how they were going to cope with being separated for the next four months. "After dinner."

They were hit with a barrage of birdseed on their way out the door. They laughed and tried to catch it in their outstretched hands.

"Pictures," Helen insisted, and when Summer groaned, she added, "Just a few more. That's all."

"Mother, you'll get plenty of pictures later."

"I want some now," her mother insisted. But "some" turned out to be at least a hundred by James's estimation.

They signed the marriage license, and James took the opportunity to kiss his bride. "I don't ever want to spend another day like this one," he whispered.

"Me, neither," she said, then giggled. "But you're going to get something out of it. Mother bought me this cute little black nightie."

James could feel the hot blood circle his ears and . . . other places. "Your mother bought you a nightie?"

"She said it's her wedding gift to you."

"I'll thank her later."

"Wait until you see what Julie got us," she whispered.

"I have the feeling it isn't a toaster," he said wryly.

Summer laughed. "No. She picked it out when Mom wasn't looking. You do like tassels, don't you?"

"Tassels?"

"Shh." Summer looked around to be sure no one was listening. "I'll save them for after the honeymoon."

"Why?"

"Because, my darling husband, they cover—" She stopped abruptly.

"Yes?" he coaxed.

"Husband," she said the word as if saying a prayer. "James, you're my *husband.*"

"I know. And you're my wife." It hit him then, too. The beauty of it, of belonging to each other, of the word itself.

Their families all seemed to return at once.

"I don't know about anyone else," Helen Lawton was saying, "but I'm starved."

There was a chorus of agreement. They trooped into the hotel's elegant restaurant and ordered dinner and champagne, although Summer could barely eat and had trouble following the conversation.

"We'll say good-night, then," James announced the minute they could leave without being rude. "Thank you all for making this the most incredible day of my life."

"It's still early," Helen protested.

. "Helen," Hank snapped. "Think about it."

"Oh, yes, sorry." Helen's face brightened, and she smiled apologetically at James.

"Will we see you in the morning?"

"Helen!" her husband growled.

"I'm just asking, Hank. What harm is there in asking?"

"I don't know, Mom. What time is your flight?"

James didn't listen to the answer, although he supposed he should have. As it was, he had a hard time hiding his impatience. He and his wife—his wife—would only have two more days together. Luckily that was two days and *three* nights. Their flights were leaving within a half hour of each other, and then it would be a whole month before he saw her again.

"All right, then, darling," Helen said, hugging Summer, "we'll see you both in the morning."

The entourage left, and James was alone with Summer at last.

"Are we going to my room or yours?" she asked, smiling up at him.

"Neither. I rented the honeymoon suite here for the rest of our stay. Your mother packed your suitcase and had it sent over."

"You think of everything." She reached up and removed the wedding veil and shook her head, freeing her curls. "I can't tell you how anxious I am to get out of this dress."

James chuckled as he led the way to the elevator. "Not nearly as anxious as I am to get you out of it."

"Who were all those guests?" she asked him when they stepped inside the elevator car.

"I thought they were friends of your family."

"I've never seen them before in my life."

James shrugged. "Me, neither."

"You know what? I'll bet my mother invited them. She couldn't bear to have us married in an empty chapel."

James fingered his room key. "Are you hungry?"

"No."

"Good. Let's go work up an appetite."

Summer smiled and moistened her lips with the tip of her tongue. "I have a feeling you aren't talking about racquetball."

James cleared his throat. He wanted her so much his body trembled with the strength of his need. "You're right about that."

Six

James astonished Summer. She didn't know what to expect from him as a lover, but it wasn't this. They'd made love no less than three times during their wedding night, and Summer woke the following morning to find him standing at the foot of their bed, fresh from the shower.

His nude body glistened in the early-morning light. Droplets of water dripped from his hair and onto the dark curls that covered his chest.

"Good morning, Mrs. Wilkens."

Summer smiled and stretched her arms high above her head, arching her back. The sheet slipped away, exposing her breasts.

"Good morning, James." She saw that he was fully aroused and slowly lifted her gaze to his. Already her body was responding to him, throbbing with readiness and need. James's eyes narrowed as they focused on her.

Wordlessly she knelt on the bed and held out her

arms to him. She smiled, thinking someone should've warned her about this man before they were married. At this rate, they'd both be dead within a week.

He walked over to the side of the bed, kissed her once, twice, and then knelt beside it.

All her life Summer had never experienced such power. Or such love. Her breathing grew slow and shallow. She half closed her eyes in pleasure at the simple touch of his hand.

James groaned, and Summer recognized his meaning. He couldn't wait any longer. Neither could she. She threw her arms around his neck and slowly lay back against the bed, bringing him with her.

She smiled contentedly as they began to make love. All of a sudden her eyes flew open. "James, you forgot—"

"It'll be all right," he assured her breathlessly. "Just this one time."

She didn't want him to stop. Not now. "Okay."

James reached his climax soon after she experienced hers. A harsh groan tore from his throat, and his powerful body shuddered.

His shoulders still heaving, he gathered her in his arms and spread soft, delicate kisses over her face. He started to move away from her, but she wouldn't let him.

"Not yet," she pleaded. "I want to be a part of you."

"You are. You always will be. You could travel to Mars, and my heart would be with you." He brushed the damp hair from her forehead. "I can't believe you love me."

"I do, so much my heart feels like it's about to burst wide open. Will it always be like this?" she asked. "Two weeks ago, you were someone whose letters I looked forward to. This week you're the most important person in my life."

James kissed the tip of her nose. "It's only going to get better from here on out."

"Better?" She laughed delightedly. "I can't imagine it."

In one uninterrupted movement James rolled onto his back, taking her with him so she was sprawled across his chest. Across his heart. "I can't, either. Summer, I love you."

"Good." She pressed her head against his shoulder. "But what about—"

"I'll remember next time," he promised. "The last thing we need now is an unplanned pregnancy."

"I'm pretty sure this is my safe time, so don't worry."

James kissed her neck. "I suppose we should get dressed and meet everyone for breakfast."

"I suppose," she agreed, but neither of them showed any signs of moving.

"It won't be so bad," James whispered.

They'd been married less than twenty-four

hours and already Summer could read her husband's thoughts. "Being separated? It's going to be terrible. I don't know how I'll last four months without you."

"Four months." He made it sound like an eternity.

"James, where do you live?"

He gave her a puzzled look. "Seattle. You know my address."

"But is it an apartment? A condo? A town house or what?"

"A house."

Summer liked the idea of that.

A slow grin spread across his face. "I must've known I was going to meet you. This is a big house on Queen Anne Hill with seven bedrooms."

"James!"

"It's a lovely older home. I'm quite proud of the garden. I hope you'll like it."

"I love it already."

"You haven't seen it."

"No, but I saw the look on your face when you talked about it. The house is going to be perfect for us, just perfect."

His eyes grew dark. "*You're* perfect."

"I hope we'll always love each other as much as we do at this moment." Summer laid her head on his chest and sighed.

Time had never passed more quickly for James. He'd dreaded leaving Summer almost from the moment they'd met again on New Year's Eve. It was as though Seattle was another world, one he wasn't that eager to return to. Not when it meant having to say goodbye to Summer.

His wife of two days was unusually quiet as they packed their suitcases on Saturday morning, the day of their departure. When she found him watching her, she offered him a reassuring smile.

The bellboy carried their luggage to the lobby. While James was checking out of the hotel, he noticed Summer twisting the plain gold band around her finger. His own felt awkward and heavy, and he wondered if she was experiencing any regrets. For his own part, he didn't have a single one.

Having returned the rental car earlier, James ordered a car. He and Summer held hands as they rode silently to the airport.

He wanted to assure her it wouldn't be so bad, but that would've been a blatant lie. Every minute he was away from her was a minute too long. He wanted to be sure she understood how much he loved her, how crucial she was to him. But the backseat of a limo with a driver listening in didn't seem the most appropriate place to tell her those things.

Nothing would ever be the same for either of them, and they both knew it.

The car dropped them off, and since they were flying on different airlines, they separated to check in their luggage and receive their seat assignments.

James finished first and caught sight of Summer hurrying through the crowd toward him. Even from that distance he sensed her sadness. He met her halfway and they went through security together.

"My flight leaves from Concourse B," she said, looking down at her ticket. Her voice was small and tight.

"Mine's Concourse A."

"What time's your flight?"

She already knew, but apparently needed to hear it again. "Ten-thirty," James told her.

"My departure's at ten."

He was perfectly aware of what time her plane left. "I'll walk down to Concourse B with you."

"You can't, James, you might miss your own flight."

Frankly he didn't give a damn. "Then I'll catch the next one."

"I'll worry. James, really, I'm a big girl. I can find my way around the airport."

"I didn't say you couldn't," he snapped, surprising himself.

Summer looked up at him, her eyes brimming with tears. She turned and walked away from him and headed for Concourse B.

James followed and wanted to kick himself. He wouldn't see his wife for weeks and here he was, apparently doing his utmost to start an argument. No doubt there was some psychological reason for his attitude. He'd examine what was happening later, but at the moment he was more concerned about saying goodbye to her properly.

Summer arrived at her gate and walked over to the window. James could see her plane and knew it wouldn't be more than a few moments before the boarding call was announced.

"I'm sorry, sweetheart." He rested his hands on her shoulders and closed his eyes.

"Me, too."

He frowned. She'd done nothing wrong. "For what?"

"Oh, James," she whispered brokenly, slipping her arms around his waist. "I'm going to be so lost without you."

"It's going to be hard." He wasn't willing to pretend otherwise. "I'll phone as often as I can."

"Do you have my work schedule?" she asked.

"Yes. Do you have everything you need?" They'd gone over the details a dozen times.

"No. I need you, James."

His hold on her tightened. He wondered if they were afraid they'd lose the magic. Afraid that once they returned to their respective lives, everything would change.

Her flight number was announced, and James tensed. It wouldn't be long before he saw her, he promised himself. He'd try for a week, two at the most. A few minutes later her row was called.

"That's you," he said reluctantly.

"I know."

But neither of them made a move to break apart.

Summer was the last one to board the plane, and James had to tear through the airport in order to catch his own flight. If anyone had suggested even ten days ago that the dignified James Wilkens would race through an airport so he could spend a few extra minutes with a woman, he would have scoffed. He wasn't scoffing now.

He arrived in the nick of time and collapsed into his seat, his heart racing.

Between dashing through airports and hours spent making love, Summer would be the death of him yet. He smiled as he snapped his seat belt into place. If he was to die that very moment, he'd leave this earth a happy man.

James's house had never seemed so empty. By the time he got home, it was dark and shadowy. His first mistake had been stopping at the office on his way back from the airport. After he arrived in Seattle, he'd spent what remained of the day working through the memos, briefs and case histories. No one else was in, so he was able to accomplish quite a bit, catching up on some of his backlog. He'd do anything he had to so he could arrange time away as soon as possible.

Summer was never far from his thoughts.

Once he reached his house, suitcase in hand, he was exhausted. He switched on the light in the kitchen, put down his bags and set his briefcase on the walnut table in the breakfast nook.

He hadn't eaten since that morning, and a look inside the refrigerator reminded him he'd been away all week. He'd need to order out or microwave something from the freezer.

Deciding against both, he heated a can of soup, ate, then showered. He'd showered that morning, but Summer had been in the stall with him and neither one had seemed particularly concerned about washing.

James stood in front of the mirror in the steamy bathroom and wiped off some of the condensation, then stared at his reflection. He didn't look all that different from the man he'd been a week ago. But he *was* different.

Unable to delay talking to Summer, he dressed quickly and headed for his book-lined den.

Having memorized her apartment and cell phone numbers, James called her at home.

Summer answered on the first ring. "Hello."

"Hello, darling."

"James!"

"I would've called sooner, but I went to the office. I needed to clear off my desk."

"Did you check your calendar?"

"First thing. I can fly down on a Saturday

morning in two weeks, but I'll need to be back Sunday afternoon. That doesn't give us much time."

"No," she agreed, "but we'll make the most of it." Her relief was evident. "I was afraid once you looked at your schedule you'd find it impossible to get away."

"I don't care what it takes, I'll be in California in two weeks."

"Wonderful. I traded weekends with a friend so I can come to you in February. My mother's already started to plan the wedding. She's left a message with the secretary at the Moose Hall. It's a very nice building."

"Your mother's enjoying every minute of this, isn't she?"

Summer laughed. "Yes. But the one who surprises me most is my dad. I don't know what you said or did, but my dad thinks you walk on water."

It was his turn to laugh.

Then they were both silent. They'd spent nearly every minute of the previous week together. They'd discussed everything there was to discuss. Yet neither was willing to break the connection.

An hour later they were still on the phone. They hadn't spoken more than a few words between whispered promises and deep sighs. They'd shared a few secrets and memories, some of them very private. Very intimate . . .

In their next conversation, he'd let Summer know he couldn't handle much more of that.

"I've gotten together with a group of businessmen and spread the word," Ralph Southworth was saying.

James sat in his office, gazing into the distance. As always, his thoughts were fifteen hundred miles to the south with Summer. He barely heard his campaign manager. In eight days he'd be with his wife. The last six had been the purest form of torture.

He lived for the times he could phone her. Because she performed in the last show of the night, he couldn't reach her until after ten, and more often than not they spoke until past midnight.

"There's a dinner party this Friday night at the Morrisons'," Ralph announced.

James didn't comment.

"You're going, aren't you?"

"You mean to the Morrisons'?"

Ralph Southworth looked at him oddly. "Who else do you think I mean?"

James shrugged. Ralph was a good man, a bit abrasive at times, but sincere and hardworking. According to people James trusted, Ralph Southworth was the best man for the job of getting James elected to the superior court.

"What's with you lately, James?" Ralph asked

abruptly. He pulled out a chair and sat down across from James's desk.

Ralph was nothing if not direct. "What makes you ask?"

"Something's not right. Ever since you got back from vacation, you haven't been the same."

James considered telling Ralph the truth. Part of him was eager to share the news of his marriage. Marrying Summer was nothing to be ashamed of—the opposite, in fact—but arrangements for the second ceremony were already being made. If he was willing to face the truth, James would have to admit he wasn't keen on explaining his sudden marriage, especially to the man who'd frowned on his vacation in Vegas. He preferred to leave things as they were and invite Ralph to the wedding in April. So far, he'd told no one about Summer and for the time being even left his wedding band at home.

"Have you ever been in love?" he asked, unable to resist.

Ralph shook his head adamantly. "Never, and proud of it."

James's eyebrows shot to his hairline. "I see."

"Women have ruined more than one good man. Don't be a fool, James. Don't do anything stupid at this point. Unless it's with someone who can help you politically, of course. Now, if you told me you were seeing Mary Horton . . ."

"Who?"

"Mary Horton—never mind, she's not your type. All I can say is that if you're going to fall for someone now, just make sure it's a woman who can help you politically."

"She can't."

Ralph tossed his hands in the air. "Somehow, I knew you were going to say that. Listen. Keep your head screwed on tight and your pants zipped up. The last thing we need now is a scandal, understand?"

"Of course. Summer's not like—"

"Her name is *Summer?*" Ralph rolled his eyes expressively. "James, listen to me. You've asked me to run your campaign, and I'm glad to do it, but I'm telling you right now, getting involved with a woman named Summer is asking for trouble."

"Don't you think you're being unfair?"

"No. Where'd you meet her?"

"Vegas."

Ralph's mouth thinned. "Don't tell me she's a show girl," he muttered.

"No—but she's an actress."

A muscle leapt in his friend's jaw. "Don't say anything more. Not a single word. I've got high blood pressure and don't want to know any more than you've already told me."

"Summer has nothing to do with you," James said, finding it difficult to quell his irritation. Ralph made Summer sound like . . . like a mistake.

"Don't you remember a certain congressman who got involved with a stripper a few years back?"

"Summer isn't a stripper!"

"It ruined him, James. Ruined him. I don't want the same thing to happen to you."

"It won't. Furthermore, I won't have you speaking about her in those terms." In light of Ralph's reaction, James didn't think now was the time to announce they were already married. "If you must know, I intend to marry her."

"Great. Do it after the election."

"We've decided on April."

"April!" Ralph barked. "That's much too soon. Listen, you're paying me big money to run this campaign. You want my advice, you've got it. What difference would a few months make?" He paused, waiting for James's response. "Will you do that one thing?"

"I don't know."

"Are you afraid you'll lose her?"

"No."

"Then put off the wedding until after the election. Is that so much to ask?"

"I'm not sure which is worse," Julie said, applying bright red polish to her toenails, "this year or last."

"What do you mean?" Summer asked.

"You." She swirled the brush in the red paint and started with the little toe on her left foot. "Last year, after you broke up with Brett, you moped around the apartment for months."

Summer laughed. "This year isn't much better, is it?"

"Not that I can see. Listen, I understand how much you miss James. The guy's hot. No wonder you fell for him. If the situation was reversed, you can bet I'd be just as miserable. The thing is, you won't be apart for long. April's right around the corner."

Summer folded her arms and leaned against the back of the sofa. "I didn't know it was possible to love someone as much as I love James."

"If the number of times he calls you is any indication, I'd say he feels the same about you."

"He works so hard." Summer knew that many of James's late-night calls came from his office. She also knew he was putting in extra-long hours in order to free up time he could spend with her.

"Summer, he'll be here in a few days."

"I know."

"You haven't told him about Brett?" Julie asked.

Summer's nails bit into her palms. "What good would it do? James is fifteen hundred miles away. Brett hasn't got a chance with me. Unfortunately he doesn't seem ready to accept that. But he's going to get the same message whenever he calls."

"By the way, when James visits, I'm out of here."

"Julie, you don't need to leave. We can get a hotel room—really, we don't mind."

"Don't be ridiculous. This is your home. You'd be more relaxed, and both of you have been through enough stress lately."

Summer was so grateful it was all she could do not to weep. It was the stress, she decided, this tendency to be over emotional. "Have I told you how glad I am that you're my friend?"

"Think nothing of it," Julie said airily.

"I mean it, Julie. I don't know what I would've done without you these last weeks. I feel like my whole world's been turned upside down."

"It has been. Who else goes away for a week and comes home married? Did you think James had lost his mind when he suggested it?"

"Yes," she admitted, remembering the most fabulous dinner of her life. "I don't think he's done anything that impulsive his whole life."

Julie grinned. "Until he met you."

"Funny, James made the same comment."

The phone rang just then, and Summer leapt up to answer it on the off chance it was James.

"Hello," she said breathlessly.

"Summer, don't hang up, please, I'm begging you."

"Brett." Her heart sank. "Please," she told him, "just leave me alone."

"Talk to me. That's all I'm asking."

"About what? We have absolutely nothing to say to each other."

"I made a mistake."

Summer closed her eyes, fighting the frustration. "It's too late. What do I have to say to convince you of that? You're married, I'm married."

"I don't believe it." His voice grew hoarse. "If you're married, then where's your husband?"

"I don't owe you any explanations. Don't phone me again. It's over and has been for more than a year."

"Summer, please . . . please."

She didn't wait to hear any more. His persistence astonished her. When she'd found him with another woman, he'd seemed almost glad, as though he was relieved to be free of the relationship. In retrospect, Summer realized that Brett had fallen out of love with her long before, but had lacked the courage to say anything. Later, when he'd married, and she learned it wasn't the same woman he'd been with in Vegas, she wondered about this man she thought she knew so well, and discovered she didn't know him at all.

His behavior mystified her. After loving Brett for six years, she expected to feel *something* for him, but all the feeling she could muster was pity. She wanted nothing to do with him. He'd made his choice and she'd made hers.

"Brett? Again?" Julie asked when Summer joined her in the living room.

Summer nodded. "I hope this is the end of it."

"Have you thought about having the phone number changed?"

"That's a good idea. And I'm going to get call display, too."

Julie studied her for a moment. "Are you going to tell James why we've got a new phone number?"

"No. It would only worry him, and there's nothing he can do so far away. Brett doesn't concern me."

"Maybe he should."

Summer arrived at the Orange County airport forty minutes before James's flight was due, in case it came in early. Every minute of their day and a half together was carefully planned.

The only negative for Summer was the brunch with her parents Sunday morning. Her mother had several questions about the wedding that she needed to discuss with James. Summer begrudged every minute she had to share James; she knew she was being selfish, but she didn't care.

Julie, true to her word, had made a weekend trip to visit a family member, an elderly aunt in Claremont.

By the time James's plane touched down, she was nearly sick to her stomach with anticipation. As soon as he stepped out of the secure area, he paused, searching for her.

Their eyes connected and in the second before he started toward her, her heart seemed to stop. Then it began to race.

When they'd parted in Las Vegas, it felt as if everything had come to an abrupt standstill. Now she could see him, could *feel* him, for the first time since they'd parted two weeks ago.

Dashing between the other passengers, she ran toward him. James caught her in his arms and crushed her against him. His hands were in her hair, and his mouth hungrily sought hers.

His embrace half lifted her from the ground. She clung to him, fighting back a flood of emotion. Unexpectedly tears filled her eyes, but she was too happy to care.

James broke off the kiss, and Summer stared up at him, smiling. It was so good to see him.

"What's this?" he asked, brushing his thumb across the moisture on her cheeks.

"I guess I missed you more than I realized."

"You're beautiful," he said in a low voice.

"I bet you tell all the women that," she joked.

"Nope, only the ones I marry."

Summer slipped her arm around his waist, and together they headed toward the luggage carousel. "I packed light."

"Good." Because it felt so good to be close to him, she stood on the tips of her toes and kissed his cheek. "You'll be glad to hear Julie's gone for the weekend."

"Remind me to thank her."

"She's been wonderful."

"Any more crank calls?"

Summer had almost forgotten that was the excuse she'd given him when she'd had her phone numbers changed. "None." And then, because she was eager to change the subject, she told him, "I've got every minute planned."

"Every minute?"

"Well, almost. Mom and Dad invited us over for brunch in the morning. I couldn't think of any way to get out of it."

"It might be a good idea to see them."

"Why?"

James frowned, and she noticed the dark circles under his eyes. He was working too hard, not sleeping enough, not eating properly. That would all change when she got to Seattle. The first thing she'd do was make sure he had three decent meals a day. As for time in bed, well, she didn't think that would be a problem.

"There might be a problem with the wedding date," he said reluctantly.

Summer halted midstep. "What do you mean?"

"April might not work, after all." He paused. "It doesn't matter, does it? We're already married."

"I know, but . . ."

"We can talk about it later, with your family. All right?"

She nodded, unwilling to waste even one precious minute arguing over a fancy wedding when she already wore his ring.

Seven

For years James had lived an impassive and sober life. He'd never considered himself a physical man. But three weeks after marrying Summer, making love occupied far more of his thoughts than it had in the previous thirty-odd years combined.

"How far is it to your apartment?" he asked, as they walked to her car.

Summer didn't immediately respond.

"Summer?"

"It seems to me we have a few things to discuss."

"All right," he said, forcing himself to stop staring at her. She had him at a distinct disadvantage. At the moment he would have agreed to just about anything, no matter where the discussion led—as long as they got to her place soon. As long as they could be alone . . .

"I want to know why there's a problem with the wedding date."

He should've realized. "Sweetheart, it has more to do with your parents than you and me. Let's not worry about it now."

"You want to delay the wedding, don't you?"

"No," he responded vehemently. "Do you honestly think I'm enjoying this separation? I couldn't be more miserable."

"Me, neither."

"Then you have to believe I wouldn't do anything that would keep us apart any longer than necessary." James glanced at her as she drove. He was telling the truth, although not, perhaps, the whole truth. Time enough for that later, he thought. He was worried about Summer. She seemed pale and drawn, as if she weren't sleeping well or eating right. This situation wasn't good for either of them.

After fifteen minutes they arrived at her apartment building. He carried in his suitcase and set it down in her small living room, gazing around.

Summer's personality seemed to mark each area. The apartment was bright and cheerful. The kitchen especially appealed to him; the cabinets had been painted a bold yellow with red knobs. Without asking, he knew this was her special touch.

She led him into her bedroom, and he stopped when he noticed the five-foot wall poster of her as Beauty posing with the Beast. She looked so beautiful he couldn't take his eyes off it. He felt a hint of jealousy of the man who was able to spend time with her every night, even if it was in costume.

His gaze moved from the picture to the bed. A single. He supposed it wouldn't matter. The way he felt just then, they'd spend the whole night making love anyway.

He turned toward his wife. She smiled softly, and in that instant James knew he couldn't wait any longer. His need was so great that his entire body seemed to throb with a need of its own.

He held out his hand, and she walked toward him.

If he had any regrets about their time in Vegas, it was that he'd been so eager for her, so awkward and clumsy. Tonight would be slow and easy, he'd promised himself. When they made love, it would be leisurely so she'd know how much he appreciated her. They'd savor each other without interruption.

"Summer, I love you." He lifted the shirt over her head and tossed it carelessly aside. His hands were at the snap of her jeans, trembling as he struggled to hold back the urgency of his need.

He kissed her with two weeks' worth of pent-up hunger, and all his accumulated frustration broke free.

He eased the jeans over her slender hips and let them fall to her feet, then released her long enough to remove his own clothes. As he was unbuttoning his shirt, he watched her slip out of her silky underwear. His breath caught in his throat.

When James finished undressing, they collapsed on the narrow bed together. And then he lost all sense of time. . . .

. . .

Summer woke to the sound of James humming off-key in the kitchen. The man couldn't carry a tune in a bucket, as her dad liked to say. Smiling, she glanced at her clock radio—almost 6:00 p.m. She reached for her housecoat and entered the kitchen to find him examining the contents of her refrigerator.

"So you're one of those," she teased, tying the sash of her robe.

"One of what?" He reappeared brandishing a chicken leg.

"You get hungry after sex," she whispered.

"I didn't eat on the plane, and yes," he said, grinning shyly at her, "I suspect you're right."

She yawned and sat on the bar stool. "Anything interesting in there?"

"Leftover chicken, cottage cheese three weeks past its expiration date, Swiss cheese and an orange."

"I'll take the orange." She yawned again.

"Have you been getting enough sleep?" He peeled the orange and handed it to her, frowning. It wasn't his imagination; she was pale.

"More than ever. I seem to be exhausted lately. All I do is work and sleep."

"Have you seen a doctor?"

"No. I'm fine," she said, forcing a smile. She didn't want to waste their precious time together discussing her sleeping patterns. She ate a section of the rather dry orange. "I better shower and get dressed."

"For the show?"

She nodded, sad that part of her weekend with James would be spent on the job, but there was no help for it. It was difficult enough to trade schedules in order to fly up to Seattle.

"I'm looking forward to seeing what a talented woman I married."

"I hope I don't disappoint you."

"Not possible." He shook his head solemnly.

"James," she said, staring down at the orange. "Do you ever wonder what's really there between us?"

He tossed the chicken bone into the garbage. "What do you mean?"

"Sometimes I'm afraid all we share is a strong physical attraction. Is there more?"

He swallowed; the question seemed to make him uncomfortable. "What makes you ask that?"

"In case you haven't noticed, we can't keep our hands off each other."

"What's wrong with that?"

"I think about us making love—a lot. Probably more than I should. You're a brilliant man. I'm fairly sure you didn't marry me because I challenge you intellectually."

"I married you because I fell in love with you."

He made it sound so uncomplicated.

"I love the way a room lights up when you walk

into it," he said. "When you laugh, I want to laugh, too. I've never heard you sing or seen you perform on stage, but there's music in you, Summer. I sensed it the first night we met.

"Just being with you makes me want to smile. Not that you're telling jokes or doing pratfalls or anything—it's your attitude. When I'm with you, the world's a better place."

Summer felt her throat tighten.

"Like your father, an attorney or a judge can develop a jaded perspective in life. It's difficult to trust when the world's filled with suspicion. It's difficult to love when you deal with the consequences of hate every day. Perhaps that's been my problem all along."

"Not trusting?"

"Yes. You came to me without defenses, devastated, vulnerable, broken. I'd been hurt, too, so I knew how you felt because I'd experienced those same emotions. I'd walk through the fires of hell before I'd allow anyone to do that to you again." He walked over and held out his hand. "It's more than just words when I say I love you, Summer. It's my heart, my whole heart."

She gripped his hand with both of hers.

"If you're afraid our relationship is too much about sexual attraction, then maybe we should put a hold on anything physical for the rest of the weekend. Instead, we'll concentrate on getting to know each other better."

"Do you think it's possible?" She gave him a knowing look, then leaned forward. The front of her robe gaped open, and Summer watched as he stared at her breasts, then carefully averted his eyes.

"It's possible," he said in a low voice. "Not easy, but possible."

"I need to take a shower before I leave for work." She slipped off the stool and started to walk away. Then she turned, looked over her shoulder and smiled seductively. "Remember what fun we had in the shower, James?"

James paled. "Summer," he warned through clenched teeth. "If we're going to stay out of the bedroom, I'll need your help."

She turned to face him full on. "The shower isn't in the bedroom."

"Go have your shower," he said stiffly. "I'll wait for you here."

"You're sure?" She released the sash and let the silk robe fall open.

He made a sound that could mean various things—but he didn't make a move. Feeling slightly disappointed, Summer walked slowly into the bathroom and turned on the shower.

She'd just stepped inside and adjusted the water when the shower door was pulled open.

Naked, James joined her there. "You know I can't resist you," he muttered.

"Yes," she said softly. "I can't resist you, either."

. . .

Summer and her mother were busy in the kitchen at the Lawton family home. James sat in the living room with his father-in-law, watching a Sunday-morning sports show.

James didn't have the heart to tell Hank that he didn't follow sports all that much. And he sure wasn't going to admit he found them boring.

"Helen's going to be talking to you later," Hank said, relaxing during a spell of uninterrupted beer commercials. "She's having trouble getting a decent hall for the wedding reception in April. The church is no problem, mind you, but finding a hall's become pretty complicated."

"Summer said something about the Moose Hall."

"That fell through. I'll let Helen do the explaining."

"Does Summer know this?"

"Not yet. Couldn't see upsetting her. The girl's been miserable ever since she got back from Vegas. You want my opinion?" He didn't wait for a response. "You should take her to Seattle with you now and be done with it. It's clear to me the two of you belong together."

James wished it was that easy.

"I know, I know," Hank said, scooting forward to the edge of his chair as some football players ran back onto a muddy field. "She has to fulfill her contract. Never understood where the girl got her singing talent."

"She's fabulous." Summer's performance had shocked James. Her singing had moved him deeply and her acting impressed him.

Hank beamed proudly. "She's good, isn't she? I'll never forget the night I first went to see her perform at Disneyland. It was all I could do not to stand up and yell out, 'Hey, that's my little girl up there.'"

"There's such power in her voice."

"Enough to crack crystal, isn't it? You'd never suspect it hearing her speak, but the minute she opens her mouth to sing, watch out. I've never heard anything like it."

James had come away awed by her talent. That she'd willingly walk away from her career to be his wife, willingly take her chances in a new city, humbled him.

"She could go all the way to the top."

Hank nodded. "I think so, too, if she wanted, but that's the thing. She loves singing, don't get me wrong, but Summer will be just as happy humming lullabies to her babies as she would be performing in some hit Broadway show."

James's heart clutched at the thought of Summer singing to their children.

"Helen's mother used to sing," Hank said, but his eyes didn't leave the television screen. He frowned when the sports highlights moved on to tennis. "Ruth didn't sing professionally, but she was a member of the church choir for years.

Talent's a funny business. Summer was singing from the time she was two. Now, Adam, he sounds like a squeaky door."

"Me, too." All James could hope was that their children inherited their mother's singing ability.

"Don't worry about it. She loves you anyway."

James wasn't quite sure how to respond, but fortunately he didn't have to, because Helen poked her head in at that moment.

"Brunch is ready," she said. "Hank, turn off that blasted TV."

"But, Helen—"

"Hank!"

"All right, all right." Reluctantly Hank reached for the TV controller and muted the television. His wife didn't seem to notice, and Hank sent James a conspiratorial wink. "Compromise," he whispered. "She won't even know."

James sat next to Summer at the table. "This looks delicious," he said to Helen. His mother-in-law had obviously gone to a lot of trouble with this brunch. She'd prepared sausages and ham slices and bacon, along with some kind of egg casserole, fresh-baked sweet rolls, coffee and juice.

Helen waited until they'd all filled their plates before she mentioned the April wedding date. "The reason I wanted to talk to the two of you has to do with the wedding date." She paused, apparently unsure how to proceed. "I wasn't too involved with Adam's wedding when he married Denise. I had no idea we'd need to book the reception hall so far in advance."

"But I thought you already *had* the place," Summer wailed.

"Didn't happen, sweetheart," Hank said. "Trust me, your mother's done her best. I can't tell you how many phone calls she's made."

"If we're going to have the wedding you deserve," her mother said pointedly, "it'll need to be later than April. My goodness, it takes time just to get the invitations printed, and we can't order them until we have someplace *nice* for the reception."

"How much later?" was James's question.

Helen and Hank exchanged looks. "June might work, but September would be best."

"September," Summer cried.

"September's out of the question." With the primary in September, James couldn't manage time away for a wedding. "If we're going to wait that long, anyway, then let's do it after the election in November." The minute he made the suggestion, James realized he'd said the wrong thing.

"November." Summer's voice sagged with defeat. "So what am I supposed to do between April and November?"

"Move up to Seattle with James, of course," Hank said without a qualm.

"Absolutely not," Helen protested. "We can't have our daughter living with James before they're married."

"Helen, for the love of heaven, they're already married. Remember?"

"Yes, but no one knows that."

"James?"

Everyone turned to him. "Other than my dad, no one knows I'm married, either."

Summer seemed to wilt. "It sounds like what you're saying is that you don't want me with you."

"No!" James could hear the hurt and disappointment in her voice and wished he knew some way to solve the problem, but he didn't. "You know that isn't true."

"Why is everything suddenly so complicated?" Summer asked despondently. "It seemed so simple when James and I first decided to do things this way. Now I feel as if we're trapped."

James had the same reaction. "We'll talk about it and get back to you," he told his in-laws. Both were content to leave it at that.

After brunch he and Summer took a walk around her old neighborhood. Their pace was leisurely, and she didn't say anything for a couple of blocks. She clasped her hands behind her back as if she didn't want to be close to him just then. He gave her the space she needed, but longed to put his arm around her.

"I know you're disappointed, sweetheart. So am I," he began. "I—"

"This is what you meant about problems with the April date, isn't it? The election."

"Yes, but . . ."

"I feel like excess baggage in your life."

"Summer, you *are* my life."

"Oh, James, how did everything get so messed up?"

"It's my fault," he muttered, ramming his fingers through his hair. "I was the one who suggested we go ahead with the wedding right away."

"Thank heaven. I'd hate to think how long we'd have to wait if you hadn't."

"I was being purely selfish and only a little practical. I knew I wouldn't be able to keep from making love to you much longer."

"And you're traditional enough—*gentleman* enough—to prefer to marry me first," she suggested softly.

"Something like that." She made him sound nobler than he was. He'd married her because he wanted to. Because he couldn't imagine *not* marrying her.

"As you said, the problem is the election. I had no business marrying you when I did. Not when I knew very well what this year would be like."

"The campaign?"

He nodded. "I've never been a political person, but it's a real factor in this kind of situation."

"I thought judges were nonpartisan."

"They are, but trust me, sweetheart, there's plenty of politics involved. I want to be elected, Summer, but not enough to put you through this."

She was silent again for a long moment. "One question."

"Anything."

She lowered her head and increased her pace. "Why didn't you tell anyone we're married?"

"I told my campaign manager you and I were engaged." James hesitated, selecting his words carefully.

"And?"

"And he asked me to wait until after the election to go through with the wedding. He had a number of reasons, some valid, others not, but he did say one thing that made sense."

"What?"

"He reminded me that I'm paying him good money for his advice."

"I see." She gave a short laugh that revealed little amusement. "I don't even know your campaign manager and already I dislike him."

"Ralph. Ralph Southworth. He isn't so bad."

"What will we do, James?"

"I don't know."

"Do you want me to wait until after the election to move to Seattle?"

"No," he said vehemently.

"But you have to consider Ralph's advice."

"Something like that." They walked past a school yard with a battered chain-link fence. It looked as if every third-grade class for the past twenty years had made it his or her personal goal to climb that fence.

"I've been thinking about this constantly," James told her. It had weighed down his heart for nearly two weeks, ever since his talk with Ralph. "There are no easy solutions."

"We don't need to decide right now, do we?"

"No." Actually James was relieved. At the moment he was more than willing to say the heck with it and move Summer to Seattle in April.

"Then let's both give it some thought in the next few weeks."

"Good idea." He placed one arm around her shoulders. "I've worked hard for this opportunity to sit on the bench, Summer, but it's not worth losing you."

"Losing me?" She smiled up at him. "You'd have a very hard time getting rid of me, James Wilkens, and don't you forget it."

James chuckled and kissed her lightly. It was a bittersweet kiss, reminding him that in a matter of hours he'd be leaving her again. Only this time he didn't know exactly when he could be with her again.

Summer rubbed her face against the side of his. "Not so long ago, I had to practically beg you to kiss me in public."

"That was before you had me completely twisted around your little finger." The changes she'd already wrought in his life astonished him. "I don't know what I did to deserve you, but whatever it was I'm grateful."

"Your flight leaves in less than five hours."

"I know."

"I suppose we should go back to the apartment." She looked up at him and raised her delicate eyebrows. "That's plenty of time for what I have in mind."

"Summer . . ."

"Yes, James?" She batted her eyelashes at him. He grinned. She managed to be sexy and funny simultaneously, and he found that completely endearing.

They made their farewells to her family and were soon on their way back to the apartment. There was time to make love, he decided, shower and pack. Then he'd be gone again.

Summer must have been thinking the same thing because she said, "We always seem to be leaving each other."

James couldn't even tell her it wouldn't be for long. They parked in the lot outside her apartment, but as soon as they were out of the car James knew something wasn't right. Summer tensed, her gaze on the man climbing out of the car next to theirs.

"Summer?" James asked.

"It's Brett," she said in a low voice.

"Brett?" It took James a moment to make the connection. "*The* Brett?"

Her nod was almost imperceptible.

"What's he want?"

"I don't know."

Apparently they were about to find out. He was big—football-player size—and tanned. He wore faded cutoff jeans, a tank top and several gold chains around his neck.

"Hello, Brett," Summer said stiffly.

"Summer." He turned to James. "Who's this? A friend of your father's?"

"This is my husband. Kindly leave. We don't have anything to say to each other."

"Your husband?" Brett laughed mockingly. "You don't expect me to believe *that,* do you?"

"It's true," James answered. "Now I suggest you make yourself scarce like the lady asked."

Brett planted his muscular hands on lean hips. "Says you and what army? No way am I leaving Summer."

"As I recall, you already left her," James said smoothly, placing himself between Summer and the other man. "I also remember that you got married shortly afterward. And didn't I hear, just recently, that you and your wife are expecting a baby?"

"We're separated."

"I'm sorry to hear that. Unfortunately Summer

and I are now married and she's not interested in starting anything with you."

"I don't believe that," he muttered stubbornly.

"Oh, honestly, Brett," Summer said, not concealing her impatience. "Are you such an egotist you actually think I'd want you back?"

"You love me."

"Loved," she said. "Past tense."

"Don't give me any bull about you and granddaddy here."

"Granddaddy?" she snapped. "James is ten times the man you'll ever be." She pushed in front of James and glared at her former fiancé. "You know what? Every day of my life I thank God we ended our engagement—otherwise I'd never have met James. He's taught me what loving someone really means. Which is something *you* don't have a clue about."

James had Summer by the shoulders. "It won't do any good to argue with him," he told her. He looked at Brett, who was red-faced and angry. "I think it would be best if you left."

"Stay out of this," Brett growled.

"We're married," James said, trying to add reason to a situation that was fast getting out of hand. "Nothing you say is going to change that."

Brett spit on the ground. "She's nothing but a whore anyway."

James would've walked away for almost anything. But he refused to allow anyone to speak in a derogatory way about Summer. He stepped toward Brett until they were face-to-face. "I suggest you apologize to the lady."

"Gonna make me?"

"Yes," James said. He'd been a schoolboy the last time he was in a fistfight, but he wasn't going to let this jaded, ugly man insult his wife.

Brett's hands went up first. He swung at James, who was quick enough to step aside. The second time James wasn't so fortunate. The punch hit him square in the eye, but he didn't pay attention to the pain since he was more intent on delivering his own.

"James!" Summer repeatedly screamed his name. James could vaguely hear her in the background, pleading with him to stop, that Brett wasn't worth the trouble.

The two men wrestled to the ground, and James was able to level another couple of punches. "You'll apologize," he demanded from between clenched teeth when Brett showed signs of wanting to quit.

Blood drooled from Brett's mouth, and one eye was swollen. He nodded. "Sorry," he muttered.

James released him just as the police arrived.

Eight

Summer wouldn't have believed James was capable of such anger or such violence. Part of her wanted to call him a fool, but another part wanted to tell him how grateful she was for his love and protection.

His left eye was badly swollen, even with the bag of ice she'd given him. James had refused to hold it to his face while he talked to the police.

His black eye wasn't the only damage. His mouth was cut, and an ugly bruise was beginning to form along his jaw. Brett was in much worse shape, with what looked to be a broken nose.

After talking to both Brett and James and a couple of witnesses, the police asked James if he wanted to press charges. James eyed Brett.

"I don't think that'll be necessary. I doubt this . . . gentleman will bother my wife again. Isn't that right?" he asked, turning to Brett.

Brett wiped the blood from the side of his mouth. "I didn't come here looking for trouble."

"Looks like that's what you got, though," the police officer told him. "I'd count my blessings and stay away." He studied him for a moment, then asked, "Want to go to the hospital?"

"Forget it. I'm out of here," Brett said with disgust. He climbed inside his car and slammed the door, then drove off as if he couldn't get away fast enough.

"He won't be back," Summer said confidently. She knew Brett's ego was fragile and he wouldn't return after being humiliated.

"You're right, he won't," James insisted darkly, "because you're filing a restraining order first thing tomorrow morning."

Summer nodded, wishing she'd thought of doing it earlier.

"This isn't the first time he's pestered you, is it?"

Summer lowered her gaze.

"He's the reason you had your phone number changed, isn't he?"

She gave a small nod.

"Why didn't you tell me?"

"What could you have done from Seattle?"

"You should have told me. I could at least have offered you some advice. For that matter, why didn't you tell your father?"

James was furious and she suspected she was about to receive the lecture of her life. When nothing more came, she raised her eyes to her husband—and wanted to weep.

His face was a mess. His eye was completely swollen now. It might have been better if she could've convinced him to apply the ice pack. Anyone looking at him would know instantly that her husband the judge had been involved in an altercation—and all because of her.

The police left soon afterward.

"Can I get you anything?" Summer asked guiltily as they entered the apartment.

"I'm fine," he said curtly.

But he wasn't fine. His hands were swollen, his knuckles scraped and bleeding. All at once he started to blur, and the room spun. Everything seemed to be closing in on her. Panic-stricken, Summer groped for the kitchen counter and held on until the waves of dizziness passed.

"Summer? What's wrong?"

"Nothing. I got a little light-headed, that's all." She didn't mention how close she'd come to passing out. Even now, she felt the force of her will was the only thing keeping her conscious.

James came to her and placed his arm around her waist, gently guiding her into the living room. They sat on the sofa, and Summer rested her head against his shoulder, wondering what was wrong with her.

"I'm so sorry," she whispered, fighting back tears.

"For what?"

"The fight."

"That wasn't your fault."

"But, James, you have a terrible black eye. What will people say?" She hated to think about the speculation he'd face when he returned to Seattle, and it was all on account of her. Perhaps she should've told him that Brett was bothering her, but she hadn't wanted to burden him with her troubles.

"Everyone will figure I was in a major fistfight," James teased. "It'll probably be the best thing to happen to my reputation in years. People will see me in an entirely new light."

"Everyone will wonder. . . ."

"Of course they will, and I'll tell them they should see the other guy."

Summer made an effort to laugh but found she couldn't. She twisted her head a bit so she could look at him. The bruise on his jaw was a vivid purple. She raised tentative fingers to it and bit her lip when he winced.

"Oh, James." Gently she pressed her lips to the underside of his jaw.

"That helps." He laughed and groaned at the same time.

She kissed him again, easing her mouth toward his. He moaned and before long, they were exchanging deep, hungry kisses.

"I refuse," James said, unbuttoning her blouse but having difficulty with his swollen hands, "to allow Brett to ruin our last few hours together."

She smiled and slid her arms around his shoulders. "Want to have a shower?" she breathed.

"Yes, but do you have a large enough hot-water tank?"

Summer giggled, recalling their last experience in her compact shower stall and how the water had gone cold at precisely the wrong moment.

The sound of the key turning in the lock told Summer her roommate was home. She sat back abruptly and fastened her blouse.

"Hi, everyone." Julie stepped into the living room and set her suitcase on the floor. "I'm not interrupting anything, am I?" Her gaze narrowed. "James? What on earth happened to you?"

James didn't expect his black eye to go unnoticed, but he wasn't prepared for the amount of open curiosity it aroused.

"Morning, Judge Wilkens." Louise Jamison, the assistant he shared with two other judges, greeted him when he entered the office Monday morning. Then she dropped her pencil. "Judge Wilkens!" she said. "My goodness, what happened?"

He mumbled something about meeting the wrong end of a fist and hurried into his office. It was clear he'd need to come up with an explanation that would satisfy the curious.

Brad Williams knocked on his door five minutes later. His fellow judge let himself into James's office and stared. "So it's true?"

"What's true?"

"You tell me. Looks like you've been in a fight."

"It was a minor scuffle, and that's all I'm going to say about it." James stood and reached for his robe, eager to escape a series of prying questions he didn't want to answer. He had the distinct feeling the rest of the day was going to be like this.

And he was right.

By the time he pulled out of the parking garage that evening, he regretted that he hadn't called in sick. He might've done it if a black eye would disappear in a couple of days, but that wasn't likely, so there was no point in not going in. He checked his reflection in the rearview mirror. The eye looked worse than it had the previous day. He pressed his index finger against the swelling and was surprised by the pain it caused. Still, he could live with the discomfort; it was the unsightliness of the bruises and the questions and curious glances he could do without.

Irritated and not knowing exactly whom to blame, James drove to his father's house. He hadn't been to see Walter in a couple of weeks and wanted to discuss something with him.

His father was doing a *New York Times* crossword puzzle when James let himself into the house. He looked up from the folded newspaper and did a double take, but to his credit, Walter didn't mention the black eye. "Hello, James."

"Dad."

James walked over to the snifter of Scotch Walter kept on hand and poured himself a liberal quantity. He wasn't fond of hard liquor and rarely indulged, but he felt he needed something potent. And fast.

"It's been one of those days, has it?"

James's back was to his father. "You might say that." He took his first sip and the Scotch burned its way down his throat. "This stuff could rot a man's stomach."

"So I've heard."

Taking his glass, James sat in the leather chair next to his father. "I suppose you're wondering about the eye."

"I'll admit to being curious."

"You and everyone else I've seen today."

"I can imagine you've been the object of more than one inquisitive stare."

"I was in a fistfight."

"You?"

"Don't sound so surprised. You're the one who told me there'd be times in a man's life when he couldn't walk away from a fight. This happened to be one of those."

"Want to talk about it?" His father set aside the paper.

"Not particularly, but if you must know, it was over Summer."

"Ah, yes, Summer. How is she? I'm telling you, son, I like her. Couldn't have chosen a better mate for you if I'd gone looking myself."

James smiled for the first time that day. "She's doing well. I was with her this weekend." James raised the Scotch to his lips and grimaced. "We had brunch with her parents."

"Helen and Hank. Good people," Walter commented.

"There's a problem with the April wedding date—on their end and mine. Helen suggested we wait until September. I said November, because of the election."

"Do you want that?" Walter asked.

"No. Neither does Summer."

"Then the hell with it. Let her finish out her contract with Disneyland and join you after that. You've already had a wedding. I never could understand why you wanted two ceremonies, but then I'm an old man with little appreciation for fancy weddings. What I *would* appreciate is a couple of grandkids. I'm not getting any younger, you know, and neither are you."

"Do away with the second ceremony?"

"That's what I said," Walter muttered.

James closed his eyes in relief. Of course. It made perfect sense. He'd suggested a second wedding because he thought that was what Summer wanted, but if he asked her, James suspected he'd learn otherwise. The wedding was for her parents' sake.

"How'd you get so smart?" James asked his father.

"Don't know, but I must be very wise," Walter said, and chuckled. "I've got a superior court judge for a son."

James laughed, feeling comfortable for the first time all day.

"Stay for dinner," his father insisted. "It's been a while since we spent any real time together. Afterward you can let me beat you in a game of chess, and I'll go to bed a happy man."

"All right." It was an invitation too good to refuse.

When James got home after ten, the light on his phone was blinking. He was tempted to ignore his messages.

He felt tired but relaxed and not particularly interested in returning a long list of phone calls. Especially when he suspected most of his callers were trying to learn what they could about his mysterious black eye.

The only person he wanted to talk to was Summer. He reached for the phone, and she answered on the second ring.

"I just got in," he explained. "Dad and I had dinner."

"Did you give him my love?"

"I did better than that—I let him beat me at chess."

She laughed, and James closed his eyes, savouring the melodic sound. It was like a balm after the day he'd endured.

"How's the eye?" she asked next.

"Good." So he lied. "How was the show today?"

"I didn't go in. I seem to have come down with the flu, so my understudy played Belle. I felt crummy all day. When I woke up this morning, I just felt so nauseous. At first I thought it was nerves over what happened with Brett, but it didn't go away, so I had to call in sick."

"Have you been to a doctor?"

"No. Have you?"

She had him there. "No."

"I'll be fine. I just want to be sure I didn't give you my flu bug while you were here."

"There's no sign of it," he assured her.

They must have talked for another fifteen minutes, saying nothing outwardly significant yet sharing the most important details of their lives. Their conversation would have gone on a lot longer, had someone not rung his doorbell.

It was Ralph Southworth. His campaign manager took one look at James and threw his arms dramatically in the air. "What the hell happened to you?"

"Good evening to you, too," James said evenly.

Ralph rammed all ten fingers through his hair. "Don't you listen to your messages? I've left no fewer than five, and you haven't bothered to return one."

"Sit down," James said calmly. "Do you want a drink?"

Ralph's eyes narrowed as he studied James's face. "Am I going to need it?"

"That depends." James pointed to the recliner by the large brick fireplace. He'd tell Ralph the truth because it was necessary and, knowing his campaign manager's feelings about Summer, he suspected Ralph *would* need a stiff drink. "Make yourself at home."

Instead, Ralph followed him into the kitchen. "I got no less than ten phone calls this afternoon asking about your black eye. You can't show up and then say nothing about it."

"I can't?" This was news to James, since he'd done exactly that. "I thought you were here to discuss business."

"I am." Ralph frowned when James brought an unopened bottle of top-shelf bourbon out of a cabinet. "So I'm going to need that."

"Yes."

"I met with the League of Women Voters and I've arranged for you to speak at their luncheon in July. It's a real coup, James, and I hope you appreciate my efforts."

"Yes," he murmured. "Thanks."

"Now tell me about the eye. And the bruises."

"All right," James said, adding two ice cubes to the glass. He half filled it with bourbon and handed it to his friend. "I got hit in the face with a fist more than once."

"Whose fist?"

"Some beach bum by the name of Brett. I don't remember his last name if I ever heard it."

Ralph swallowed his first sip of liquor. "Does the beach bum have anything to do with the woman you mentioned?"

"Yeah."

The two men stared across the kitchen at each other.

"Were the police called?" Ralph demanded.

It took James a moment to own up to the truth. "Yes."

Ralph slammed his hand against the counter. "I should've known! James, what did I tell you? A woman's nothing but trouble. Mark my words, if you get involved any further with Spring . . ."

"Summer!"

"Whatever. It doesn't matter, because her name spells just one thing. Trouble. You've worked all your life for this opportunity. This is your one shot at the bench. We both know it. You asked me to manage your campaign and I agreed, but I thought it would be a team effort. The two of us."

"It is." James wanted to hold on to his seat on the bench more than he'd ever wanted any-thing—other than to marry Summer. He also felt he was the best man for the position. To get this close and lose it all would be agonizing.

"Then why," Ralph asked, palms out, "are you sabotaging your own campaign?"

"I'm not doing it on purpose."

"Stay away from this woman!"

"Ralph, I can't. I won't."

Ralph rubbed his face with both hands, clearly frustrated.

"Summer's in California, but I plan on bringing her to Seattle as soon as I can arrange it. Probably April."

"Tell me you're joking."

"I'm not." James figured he should admit the truth now and be done with it. "We're married."

"What?" Ralph pulled out a chair and sank into it. "When?"

"Over New Year's."

"Why?"

"It was just . . . one of those things. We fell in love and got married. We were hoping for a more elaborate ceremony later, but I can see that's going to be a problem."

"You want to know what's the real problem, James? It's the marriage. Why didn't you tell me right away?"

"I should have," James said, sorry now that he hadn't. "But when you told me you'd never been in love, I didn't think there was much of a chance you'd understand."

"What you've done is jeopardize your entire campaign."

Somehow he doubted that. "Aren't you over-reacting?"

"Time will tell, won't it?" Ralph asked smugly.

James decided to ignore that. "If anything,

Summer will be an asset. She's lovely and she's good at connecting with people. Unfortunately her contract with Disney doesn't expire until April."

"That's right," Ralph said sarcastically. "I forgot, she's a showgirl."

"A singer and an actress and a very talented one at that," James boasted.

"An actress, a showgirl, it's all the same."

"Once she's finished with her contract, I want her to move in with me."

"Here in Seattle?" Ralph made it sound like a world-class disaster.

"A wife belongs with her husband."

"What about the beach bum?"

James frowned. "We don't have to worry about him. He's gone for good."

"I certainly hope so. And while we're making out a wish list, let's add a couple of other things. Let's wish that your worthy opponent doesn't find out about this little skirmish between you and Summer's previous lover-boy. And let's make a great big wish that he doesn't learn that the police were called and a report filed."

"He won't," James said confidently, far more confidently than he felt.

"I hope you're right," Ralph said, and downed what was left of his bourbon in one gulp. The glass hit the counter when he put it down. "Now tell me, what kind of damage did you do to the beach bum?"

"You didn't tell him, did you?" Julie said when Summer set the telephone receiver back in place.

"No." She sighed reluctantly. She rested her hand protectively on her stomach.

"A man has the right to know he's going to be a father," Julie said righteously. She bit into an apple as she tucked her feet beneath her on the sofa.

Summer closed her eyes. Even the smell of food or the sound of someone eating made her sick to her stomach. In the past two months she'd seen parts of toilets that weren't meant to be examined at such close range. She hadn't kept down a single breakfast in weeks. The day before, she'd wondered why she even bothered to eat. Dumping it directly into the toilet would save time and trouble.

"How long do you think James is going to fall for this lie about having the flu?"

It had been more than a month since she'd last seen him, and in that time Summer had lost ten pounds. Her clothes hung on her, and she was as pale as death. She seemed to spend more time at the doctor's office than she did at her own apartment. Her biggest fear was that being so ill meant there was something wrong with the baby, although the doctor had attempted to reassure her on that score.

"Why haven't you told him?" Julie wanted to know.

"I just can't do it over the phone." Besides, she remembered James mentioning that a pregnancy now would be a mistake. Well, she hadn't gotten this way by herself!

She knew exactly when it had happened, too. There was only the one time they hadn't used protection.

"When are you going to see him again?"

Summer shook her head. "I don't know."

"You talk on the phone every night. He sends you gifts. I can't think of anyone else who got six dozen red roses for Valentine's Day."

"He's extravagant. . . ."

"Extravagant with everything but his time."

"He's so busy, Julie. I never realized how much there was to being a judge, and he really cares about the people he works with. Not only the people who stand before him, but the attorneys and his staff, too. Then there's the election. . . ."

"So, go to him. He's just as unhappy without you."

"I've got three weeks left on my contract, and—"

"Do you really suppose no one's figured out that you're pregnant? Think about it, Summer. You came back from Vegas all happy and in love, and two weeks later you're heaving your guts out after every meal. No one expects you to perform when you feel this crummy."

"But . . ."

"Do everyone a favor and—" Julie stopped when there was a knock at the door. "Is anyone coming over tonight?"

"No." Summer laid her head back against the sofa and drew in several deep breaths, hoping that would ease her nausea.

"It's for you," Julie said, looking over her shoulder as soon as she'd opened the door. "It's Walter Wilkens."

Summer threw aside the blanket and scurried off the sofa, anxious to see her father-in-law. "Walter?" What could he possibly be doing here? "Come inside, please."

The refined, older gentleman stepped into the apartment. "Summer?" He gazed at her, his expression concerned. "James said you'd been ill with the flu, but my dear . . ."

"She looks dreadful," Julie finished for him. Her roommate took another noisy bite of her apple. "I'm Julie. We met at the wedding. Summer's roommate and best friend."

Walter bowed slightly. "Hello, Julie. It's nice to see you again."

"Sit down, please," Summer said, motioning toward the only chair in the house without blankets or clean laundry stacked on it.

"Would you like something to drink?" Julie asked.

"No . . . no, thank you." He cleared his throat.

"Summer, my dear." He frowned. "Have you been to a doctor?"

"Yup," Julie answered, chewing on her apple. "Three times this week, right, Summer?"

"Julie," she snapped.

"Are you going to tell him or not?"

Summer tossed the tangled curls over her shoulder and groaned inwardly. "I don't have much choice now, do I?" She met Walter's eyes and realized her lower lip was trembling. She was suddenly afraid she might burst into tears. Her emotions had been like a seesaw, veering from one extreme to another.

"Summer, what is it?" Walter prodded.

"I'm pregnant," she whispered. She smiled happily all the while tears streamed down her cheeks.

Walter bolted out of his chair. "Hot damn!"

"Other than me, you're the first person she's told," Julie felt obliged to inform him. "Not even her own family knows, although her mother would take one look at her and guess."

"James doesn't know?"

"Nope." Again it was Julie who answered.

"And why not?"

"A woman doesn't tell her husband that sort of thing over the phone," Summer insisted. "Or by e-mail." She needed to see his face, to gauge James's reaction so she'd know what he was really thinking.

"She's been sicker than a dog."

"Thank you, Julie, but I can take it from here."

"I can see that," Walter said, ignoring Summer.

"What brings you to California?" Summer asked cordially, looking for a way to change the subject.

"A business trip. I thought James might have mentioned it."

If he had, Summer had missed it. She had a feeling she'd been doing a lot of that lately.

"Well, my dear," Walter said, sitting back in his chair and grinning broadly. "This is a pleasant surprise."

"It was for me, too."

"I can just see James's face when you tell him."

"He probably won't know what to do, laugh or cry."

"He'll probably do a little of both."

Walter himself was laughing, Summer noticed. He hadn't stopped smiling from the moment he'd heard the news.

"Everything's always been so carefully planned in James's life," Walter said, still grinning. "Then he met you and bingo. He's a husband, and now he's about to be a father. This is terrific news, just terrific."

"James might not find it all that wonderful," Summer said, voicing her fears for the first time. "He's in the middle of an important campaign."

"Don't you worry about a thing."

"I *am* worried. I can't help it."

"Then we're going to have to do something about that."

"We are?" Summer asked. "What?"

"If my son's going to become a father, you should tell him, and the sooner the better. Pack your bags, Summer. It's about time you moved to Seattle with your husband where you belong."

"But . . ."

"Don't argue with me, young lady. I'm an old man and I'm accustomed to having my own way. If you're worried about his campaign, this is how we fix that. You'll be introduced to the public as his wife and we're going to put an end to any speculation right now."

Nine

Something was wrong with Summer. James had sensed it weeks ago. He would have confronted her and demanded answers if she hadn't sounded so fragile.

There was that business with the flu, but exactly how long was that going to last? When he asked her what the doctor said, she seemed vague.

Part of the problem was the length of time they'd been apart. He hadn't meant it to be so long. Summer had intended to come to Seattle, but that had fallen through, just as his last visit to California had. Neither of them was happy about it, but there was nothing James could have done on his end. He was sure that was the case with her, too.

James paced in his den, worrying. When he had to mull over a problem, that was what he did. Lately he'd practically worn a path in the carpet. He felt helpless and frustrated. Despite Ralph's dire warnings, he wished he'd brought Summer back to Seattle. This separation was hurting them both.

His greatest fear was that she regretted their marriage.

Their telephone conversations weren't the same anymore. He felt as if she was hiding something from him. They used to talk about everything but he noticed that she steered him away from certain topics now. She didn't want to talk about herself or her job or this flu that had hung on for few weeks. They used to talk for hours; now he had the feeling she was eager to get off the line.

James wondered about Brett, but when he asked, Summer assured him she hadn't seen or heard from him since the fight.

The fight.

His black eye had caused a great deal of speculation among his peers. James had never offered any explanation. Via the grapevine, he'd heard Ralph's version and found it only distantly related to the truth. According to his campaign manager, James had been jumped by gang members and valiantly fought them off until the police arrived.

When James confronted Ralph with the story, the other man smiled and said he couldn't be held accountable for rumors. Right or wrong, James had let it drop. He was eager to put the incident behind him.

James certainly hadn't expected married life to be this lonely. He'd never felt this detached from the mainstream of everyday life, this isolated. Missing Summer was like a constant ache in his stomach. Except that a store-bought tablet wasn't going to cure what ailed him.

His desk was filled with demands. He felt weary. Unsure of his marriage. Unsure of himself.

He went into the kitchen to make a cup of instant coffee when he saw a car turn into his driveway and around to the backyard.

His father.

He wondered why Walter would stop by unannounced on a Sunday afternoon. James wasn't in the mood for company—but then again, maybe a sounding board was exactly what he needed. Other than his father, there was no one with whom he could discuss Summer.

The slam of a car door closing was followed almost immediately by another. James frowned. Dad had brought someone with him. Great. Just great.

He took the hot water out of the microwave, added the coffee granules and stirred briskly. There was a knock at the back door.

"Come in, the door's open," he called, not turning around. He didn't feel like being polite. Not today, when it felt as if the world was closing in around him.

He sipped his coffee and stared out the window. The daffodils were blooming and the—

"Hello, James."

James whirled around. "Summer?" He couldn't believe she was really there. It was impossible. A figment of his imagination. An apparition. Before another second passed, James walked across the kitchen and swept her into his arms.

Laughing and sobbing at once, Summer hugged him close.

Then they were kissing each other. Neither could give or get enough.

Walter stood in the background and cleared his throat. "I'll wait for the two of you in the living room," he said, loudly enough to be sure he was heard.

As far as James was concerned, his father might as well make himself comfortable. Or leave. This could take a while.

Summer in his arms was the closest thing to heaven James had ever found. Not for several minutes did he notice how thin and frail she was. The virus had ravaged her body.

"Sweetheart," he whispered between kisses. He paused and brushed back her hair to get a good look at her.

She was pale. Her once-pink cheeks were color-less, and her eyes appeared sunken. "Are you over the flu?"

She lowered her eyes and stepped away from him. "I . . . you'd better sit down, James."

"Sit down? Why?"

Her hands closed around the back of a kitchen chair. "I have something important to tell you."

He could see she was nervous and on the verge of tears. The worries that were nipping at his heels earlier returned with reinforcements. Summer had more than a common flu bug.

"Just tell me," he said. A knot was beginning to form in his stomach. Was she ill? Was it some-thing life threatening? The knot twisted and tightened.

"I don't have the flu," she whispered.

Whatever it was, then, must be very bad if his father had brought her to Seattle.

"How serious is it?" he asked. He preferred to confront whatever they were dealing with head-on.

"It's serious, James, very serious." Slowly she raised her eyes to his. "We're going to have a baby."

His relief was so great that he nearly laughed. "A baby? You mean to tell me you're pregnant?"

She nodded. Her fingers had gone white, and she was watching him closely.

James took her in his arms. "I thought you were really sick."

"I have been really sick," she told him crisply. "Morning sickness. Afternoon sickness. Evening sickness. I . . . I can't seem to keep food down. . . . I've never been more miserable in my life."

"I suspect part of her problem has been psychological," Walter announced from the doorway. "The poor girl's been terribly worried about how you were going to take the news."

"Me?"

"My feelings exactly," Walter said. "The deed's done, what's there to think about? Besides, you've made me an extremely happy man."

"A baby." James remained awestruck at the thought.

"Now tell him your due date, Summer—he'll get a real kick out of that."

"September twenty-third," Summer announced.

Everyone seemed to be studying him, waiting for a reaction. James didn't know what to think. Then it hit him. "September twenty-third? That's the date of the primary."

"I know. Isn't it great?" Walter asked.

"How long can you stay?" James asked, taking Summer's hands in his own.

Summer looked at Walter.

"Stay?" his father barked. "My dear son, this is your wife. I brought her to Seattle to live with you. This is where she belongs."

"You can live with me?" A man could only take

in so much news at one time. First, he'd learned that his wife didn't have some life-threatening disease. Then he discovered he was going to be a father. Even more important, he was going to have the opportunity to prove what kind of husband he could be.

"Yes. I got out of my contract for medical reasons, and Julie's getting a roommate. So . . . everything's settled."

James pulled out the chair and sat Summer down. Then he knelt in front of her and took her hands in his. "A baby."

"You're sure you don't mind?"

"Of course he doesn't mind," Walter said, "and if he does I'll set up an appointment with a good psychiatrist I know. This is the best news we've had in thirty years."

"When did it happen?" James asked.

Summer laughed at him. "You mean you don't remember?" She leaned toward him and whispered, reminding him of the one episode the morning after their honeymoon night.

"Ah, yes," James said, and chuckled. "As I recall, I was the one who said one time wouldn't matter."

"I don't suppose there's anything to eat in this house?" Walter asked, banging cupboard doors open and shut.

"Why have you been so ill?" James wanted to know. It worried him. "Is it routine?"

"My doctor says some women suffer from severe morning sickness for the first few months. He's been very reassuring. I try to remember that when I'm losing my latest meal."

"Is there anything that can help?"

"She's got what she needs now," Walter said.

Summer laid her head on his shoulder. "I was worried you'd be upset with me."

"Why would I be upset when the most beautiful woman in the world tells me she's having my baby?" He reached for her hand and pressed her palm over his heart. "Notice anything different?" he asked.

She shook her head, giving him a puzzled look.

"My heart's racing because I'm so excited. Because I'm so happy. We're going to have a baby, Summer! I feel like I could conquer the world."

He wanted his words to comfort her. The last thing he expected was that she'd burst into tears.

"But you said a baby would be a mistake right now," she reminded him between sobs.

"I said that?"

"He said that?" Walter glared at James.

"I don't remember saying it," James told him. "I'm sorry, my love. Just knowing we're going to have a baby makes me happier than I have any right to be."

"Damn straight he's happy," Walter tossed in, "or there'd be hell to pay. I should've been a grandfather two or three times over by now. As far as I'm concerned, James owes me."

"I'll try and make it up to you," James promised his father with a grin.

Summer couldn't remember ever being so hungry. She'd been with James a week and had settled so contentedly into her new life it was almost as if she'd always been there.

"Would you like another piece of apple pie?" James asked. "Better yet, why don't we buy the whole thing and take it home with us?"

"Can we do that?" Summer was sure her appetite must be a source of embarrassment to him. They were at a sidewalk restaurant on the Seattle waterfront. Summer couldn't decide between the French onion soup and the Cobb salad, so she'd ordered both. Then she'd topped off the meal with a huge slice of apple pie à la mode.

"I'll ask the waitress," James said as though it was perfectly normal to order a whole pie for later.

"Have I embarrassed you?" she asked, keeping her voice low.

James's mouth quivered. "No, but I will admit I've rarely seen anyone enjoy her food more."

"Oh, James, you have no idea how good it is to be able to eat and keep everything down. I felt a thousand times better this past week than I did the whole previous two months."

"Then Dad was right," he said.

"About what?"

"The psychological effects of the pregnancy were taking their toll along with the physical. In other words, you were worried and making yourself more so. I could kick myself."

"Why?"

"For not guessing. You have to forgive me, sweetheart, I'm new to this husband business."

"You're forgiven."

"Just promise me one thing. Don't keep any more secrets from me, all right?"

She smiled. "You've got yourself a deal."

"James?" A striking-looking couple approached their table.

"Rich and Jamie Manning." Sounding genuinely pleased, James stood and exchanged handshakes with the man. Then he turned to Summer. "These are good friends of mine, Rich and Jamie Manning. This is my wife, Summer."

"Your wife?" Rich repeated, doing a poor job of hiding his surprise. "When did this happen?"

"Shortly after New Year's," James explained. "Would you care to join us?"

"Unfortunately we can't," Rich said. "The babysitter's waiting. But this is great news. I hope there's a good reason I didn't get a wedding invitation."

"A very good one." James grinned. "I've been meaning to let everyone know. But Summer just moved here from California."

"Well, the word's out now," Jamie said, smiling at her. "Once Rich's mother hears about it, she'll want to throw a party in your honor." Jamie and her husband shared a private, happy look.

"I'd better call your parents before I alienate them completely," James said.

"I'll be seeing you soon," Rich said and patted James's shoulder as he passed by. "Bye, Summer."

James was silent for a moment, and Summer wasn't sure if he was glad or not that his friends had stopped to talk. She didn't think he intended to keep their marriage a secret, yet he hadn't made a point of introducing her around, either.

"Is there a problem?" she asked.

"No. It's just that I was hoping to give you some time to regain your strength before you met my friends."

Summer's gaze followed the couple as they made their way toward the front of the restaurant.

"They're happy, aren't they?"

"Rich and Jamie?"

Summer nodded.

"Yes." He relaxed in his chair. "They came to see me a few years back with perhaps the most unusual request of my career." He smiled, and Summer guessed he must've been amused at the time, as well.

"What did they want?"

"They asked me to draw up a paper for a marriage of convenience."

174

"Really." That seemed odd to Summer. Although she'd just met the couple, it was clear to her that they were in love.

"They'd come up with some harebrained scheme to have a baby together—by artificial insemination. Rich would be the sperm donor."

"Did they have a baby?"

"Yes, but Bethany was conceived the old-fashioned way without a single visit to a fertility clinic."

Summer shook her head. "This doesn't make any sense to me. Why would two healthy people go to such lengths to have a child? Especially when they're perfectly capable of doing things . . . the usual way?"

"It does sound silly, doesn't it?"

"Frankly, yes."

James leaned forward and placed his elbows on the table. "Jamie and Rich had been friends for years. Since their high school days, if I recall correctly. Jamie couldn't seem to fall in love with the right kind of man and, after a couple of disastrous relationships, she decided she was giving up dating altogether."

"I love the tricks life plays on people," Summer said, licking melted ice cream off her spoon. She looked across the table at the remnants on James's plate. "Are you going to eat that?" she asked.

He pushed the plate toward her.

"Thanks," she said, and blew him a kiss. "Go

on," she encouraged, scooping up the last bits of pie and ice cream. "What happened?"

"Apparently Jamie was comfortable with her decision, except that she wanted a child. That's when she approached Rich about being the sperm donor."

"Just between friends, that sort of thing?"

"Exactly. At any rate, Rich didn't think it was such a bad idea himself, the not-marrying part. He'd had his own ups and downs in the relationship department. But the more he thought about her suggestion, the more problems he had with being nothing more than a sperm donor. He suggested they get married so their child could have his name. He also wanted a say in the baby's upbringing."

"And Jamie agreed to all this?"

"She wanted a child."

"So they asked you to draw up a contract or something?"

"Yes, but I have to tell you I had my reservations."

"I can imagine."

"They have two children now."

"Well, this so-called marriage of convenience certainly worked out," Summer told him.

"It sure did."

While she was looking around the table for anything left to eat, she noticed that James was studying her. "How are you feeling?" he asked.

"A thousand times better." She smiled and lowered her voice so he alone could hear. "If what
you're really asking is if I'm well enough to make
love, the answer is yes."

He swallowed hard.

"Shall we hurry home, James?"

"By all means."

He paid the tab and they were gone. "You're
sure?" he asked as he unlocked the car door and
helped her inside.

Sitting in the passenger seat, Summer smiled up
at her husband. "Am I sure? James, it's been
months since we last made love. I'm so hot for
you I could burst into flames."

James literally ran around the front of the car.
He sped the entire way home, and Summer considered it fortunate that they weren't stopped by a
traffic cop.

"Torture . . . every night for the last week,"
James mumbled as he pulled into the driveway. "I
couldn't trust myself to even touch you."

"I know."

Her time in Seattle hadn't started out well. The
first morning, she'd woken and run straight for the
bathroom. James helped her off the floor when
she'd finished. He'd cradled her in his arms and
told her how much he loved her for having their
baby.

Her first few dinners hadn't stayed down, either.
But each day after her arrival, the nausea and

episodes of vomiting had become less and less frequent. Now, one week later, she was almost herself again.

He left the car and came around to her side. When he opened the door, she stepped out and into his embrace—and kissed him.

James groaned and swung her into his arms.

"What are you doing?" she asked.

"Carrying you over the threshold," he announced. "You've been cheated out of just about everything else when it comes to this marriage."

"I haven't been cheated."

"You should've had the big church wedding and—"

"Are we going to argue about that again? Really, James, I'd rather we just made love."

He had a problem getting the door unlocked while holding her, but he managed. The minute they were inside, he started kissing her, doing wonderful, erotic things that excited her to the point of desperation.

Summer kicked off her shoes.

James kissed her and unsnapped the button to her skirt. The zipper slid down. All the while he was silently urging her toward the stairs.

Her jacket went next, followed by her shirt.

She made it to the staircase and held out her hand. James didn't need any more encouragement than that. They raced to the bedroom together.

Summer fell on the bed, laughing. "Oh, James, promise you'll always love me this much."

"I promise." He tried to remove his shirt without taking off his tie, with hilarious results. Arms clutching her stomach, Summer doubled over, laughing even harder. It was out of pure kindness that she climbed off the bed and loosened the tie enough to slip it over his head. Otherwise, she was afraid her normally calm, patient husband would have strangled himself.

"You think this is funny, do you?"

"I think you're the most wonderful man alive. Will you always want me this much?"

"I can't imagine not wanting you." And he proceeded to prove it. . . .

James was half-asleep when he heard the doorbell chime. He would have ignored it, but on the off chance it was someone important, he decided to look outside and see if he recognized the car.

Big mistake.

Ralph Southworth was at his door.

James grabbed his pants, threw on his shirt and kissed Summer on the cheek. Then he hurried down the stairs, taking a second to button his shirt before he opened the door. "Hello, Ralph," he said, standing, shoes and socks in hand.

Ralph frowned. "What the hell have you been— never mind, I already know."

"Summer's here."

"So I gather."

"Give her a few minutes, and she'll be down so you can meet her," James told him. He sat in a chair and put on his shoes and socks. "What can I do for you?"

"A number of things, but mainly I'd . . ." He hesitated as Summer made her way down the stairs. Her hair was mussed, her eyes soft and glowing.

"Ralph, this is my wife, Summer," James said proudly, joining her. He slipped his arm around her shoulders.

"Hello, Summer," Ralph said stiffly.

"Hello, Ralph."

"When did you get here?"

"Last week. Would you two like some coffee? I'll make a pot. James, take your friend into the den, why don't you, and I'll bring everything in there."

James didn't want his wife waiting on him, but something about the way she spoke told him this wasn't the time to argue. That was when he saw her skirt draped on a chair, and her jacket on the floor.

"This way, Ralph," he said, ushering the other man into the den.

He looked over his shoulder and saw Summer delicately scoop up various items of clothing, then hurry into the kitchen.

"Something amuses you?"

James cleared his throat. "Not really."

"First of all, James, I have to question your judgment. When you told me you married a show-girl—"

"Summer's an actress."

Ralph ignored that. "As I was saying, your judgment appears to be questionable."

This was a serious accusation, considering that James was running for a position on the superior court.

Ralph's lips were pinched. "It worries me that you'd marry some woman you barely know on the spur of the moment."

"Love sometimes happens like that."

"Perhaps," Ralph muttered. "Personally I wouldn't know, but James, how much younger is she?"

"Not as much as you think. Nine years."

"She's unsuitable!"

"For whom? You? Listen, Ralph, I asked you to manage my campaign, not run my life. I married Summer, and she's going to have my child."

"The girl's pregnant, as well?"

"Yes, the baby's due September twenty-third."

Ralph's lips went white with disapproval. "Could she have chosen a more inconvenient date?"

"I don't think it really matters."

"That's the primary!"

"I'm well aware of it."

"Good grief, James." Ralph shook his head. "This won't do. It just won't. Once people learn what you've done, they'll assume you were obligated to marry the girl. The last thing we need now is to have your morals questioned."

"Ralph, you're overreacting."

"I can't believe you brought her here, after everything I said."

James gritted his teeth. "She's my wife."

Ralph paced back and forth for a moment or two. "I don't feel I have any choice," he said with finality.

"Choice about what?"

"I'm resigning as your manager."

Summer appeared just then, carrying a tray. "Coffee, anyone?"

Ten

Summer settled easily into life with James. She adored her husband and treasured each moment that they were together.

Her days quickly began to follow a routine of sorts. She rose early and, because she was feeling better, resumed her regular workout, which included a two-mile run first thing in the morning.

James insisted on running with her, although he made it clear he didn't like traipsing through dark streets at dawn's early light. But he wasn't comfortable with her running alone, so he joined her, protesting every step of the way.

James was naturally athletic, and Summer didn't think anyone was more surprised than he was by how enjoyable he started to find it. After their run, they showered together. Thankfully James's hot-water tank was larger than the meager one back in her Orange County apartment.

This was both good and bad. The negative was when James, a stickler for punctuality, got to court late two mornings in a row.

"You shower first," he told her after their Monday-morning run.

"Not together?" she asked, disappointed.

"I can't be late this morning."

"We'll behave," she promised.

James snickered. "I can't behave with you, Summer. You tempt me too much."

"All right, but you shower first, and I'll get us breakfast."

Ten minutes later, he walked into the kitchen, where Summer was pouring two glasses of orange juice. He wore his dark business suit and carried his briefcase, ready for his workday.

"What are your plans?" he asked, downing the juice as he stood by the table. He sat down to eat his bagel and cream cheese and picked up the paper.

"I'm going to send Julie a long e-mail. Then I

thought I'd stop in at the library and volunteer to read during storytime."

"Good idea," he said, scanning the paper.

Summer knew reading the paper was part of his morning ritual, which he didn't have as much time for since her arrival. She drank the last of her juice and kissed his cheek.

"I'm going upstairs for my shower," she told him.

"All right. Have a good day."

"I will. Oh, what time will you be home tonight?" she asked.

"Six or so," he mumbled absently and turned the front page.

Summer hesitated. His schedule had changed. Rarely did he get home before eight the first week after she'd moved in. It seemed that every night there was someone to meet, some campaign supporter to talk to, some plan to outline—all to do with the September primary, even though it was still months away.

In the past week James had come directly home from the courthouse. Not that she was complaining, but she couldn't help wondering.

"What about your campaign?" she asked.

"Everything's under control," was all he said.

Summer wondered.

All at once James looked up, startled, as if he'd just remembered something. "What day's your ultrasound?"

"Thursday of next week. Don't look so worried. You don't need to be there."

"I *want* to be there," he stated emphatically. "Our baby's first picture. I wouldn't miss it for the world. Besides, I'm curious to find out if we're going to have a son or daughter."

"Don't tell me," she said. "I don't want to know."

"I won't," he said, chuckling. He reached out to stroke her abdomen. "I can't believe how much I love this little one, and he isn't even born yet."

"He?" she asked, hands on her hips in mock offense.

"A daughter would suit me just fine. Actually Dad's hoping for a granddaughter. It's been a long time since there's been a little girl in the family."

Summer pressed her hand over her husband's. She'd never been this happy. It frightened her sometimes. Experience had taught her that happiness almost always came with a price.

Walter joined them for dinner Wednesday evening. From the moment she'd met him, Summer had liked her father-in-law.

"Did you know Summer could cook this well when you married her?" Walter asked when they'd finished eating.

She'd found a recipe for a chicken casserole on the Internet and served it with homemade dinner rolls and fresh asparagus, with a fresh fruit salad made of seedless grapes and strawberries. For dessert she picked up a lemon torte at the local bakery.

"Summer's full of surprises," James told his father. His eyes briefly met hers.

"What he's trying to say is no one knew how fertile I was, either."

"That's the best surprise yet," Walter said. He dabbed the corner of his mouth with his napkin in a blatant effort to hide a smile.

"It certainly is," James put in.

Walter studied her. "How are you feeling these days?"

"Wonderful."

"What's the doctor have to say?"

"That I'm in excellent health. The baby's growing by leaps and bounds. I haven't felt him move yet, but—"

"Him?" James and Walter chimed in simultaneously.

"Or her," she retorted, smiling. She stood and started to clear the table.

"Let me do that," James insisted.

"I'm not helpless, you know," Walter added.

Both men leapt from their chairs.

"Go have your coffee," Summer told them. "It'll only take me a few minutes to deal with the dishes."

Walter shrugged, then looked at his son. "There

are a few things I need to discuss with James," he said.

"Then off with you." She shooed them out of the kitchen.

James poured two cups of coffee and took them into the living room. He paused in the doorway and looked over his shoulder. "You're sure?"

"James, honestly! Go talk to your father."

Although she didn't know Walter well, she sensed that something was on his mind. Throughout the meal she'd noticed the way he watched his son. James was acting odd, too.

Walter wanted to discuss the campaign, but every time he'd introduced the subject, James expertly changed it. He did it cleverly, but Walter had noticed, and after a while Summer had, too.

She ran tap water to rinse off the dinner plates before putting them in the dishwasher, and when she turned off the faucet she heard the end of James's comment.

". . . Summer doesn't know."

She hesitated. Apparently the two men didn't realize how well their voices carried. She didn't mean to eavesdrop, but it did seem only fair to listen, since she was the topic of conversation.

"What do you plan to do about it?" his father asked.

It took James a long time to answer. "I haven't decided."

"Have you tried reasoning with him?"

"No," James answered bitterly. "The man said he has doubts about my judgment. He's insulted me, insulted my wife. I don't need Southworth if he's got an attitude like that."

"But you will need a campaign manager."

"Yes," James admitted reluctantly.

So *that* was what this was about. Summer leaned against the kitchen counter and closed her eyes. Ralph had resigned, and from the evidence she'd seen, James had, too. Resigned himself to losing, even before the election. It didn't sound like him.

"What's the problem?" Walter asked as if reading Summer's mind.

James lowered his voice substantially, and Summer had to strain to hear him. "He disapproves of Summer."

"What?" Walter had no such compunction about keeping quiet. "The man's crazy!"

"I've made a series of mistakes," James said.

"Mistakes?"

"With Summer."

The world collapsed, like a house falling in on itself. Summer struggled toward a chair and literally fell into it.

"I should never have married her the way I did," James elaborated. "I cheated her out of the wedding she deserved. I don't know if her mother's forgiven me yet. The last I heard, her family's planning a reception in November. By then the baby will be here and, well, it seems a little after the fact."

"You can't blame Summer for that."

"I don't," James remarked tartly. "I blame myself. In retrospect I realize I was afraid of losing her. So I insisted on the marriage before she could change her mind."

"I don't understand what any of this has to do with Ralph," Walter muttered.

"Ralph thinks Summer's too young for me."

"Nonsense."

"He also seems to think I've done myself harm by not letting everyone know immediately that I was married. Bringing Summer here to live with me now, pregnant, and saying we've been married all along, is apparently too convenient to believe."

"It's the truth."

"You and I know that, but there's already speculation."

"So? People will always talk. Let them. But you've got to do something about getting this campaign organized. There are worse things you could be accused of than marrying in secret or getting Summer pregnant before your wedding day. As far as I'm concerned, Southworth's looking for excuses."

"I refuse to subject Summer to that kind of speculation," James said stubbornly.

"Have you talked this over with her?"

"Not yet . . ."

"You haven't?"

"I know, I know." The defeatist attitude was back in James's voice. "I've put it off longer than I should have."

After that, Summer didn't hear much more of the conversation between father and son. Their marriage had hurt her husband; it might have robbed him of his dreams, cheated him out of his goals.

The phone rang long before she had time to gather her thoughts. "I'll get it," she called out to James, and reached for the extension in the kitchen. Her hand trembled as she lifted the receiver.

"Hello," she said, her voice weak.

"Hello," came the soft feminine reply. "You don't know me. My name's Christy Manning Franklin."

"Christy . . . Manning?" Summer said, stunned. She hadn't recovered from one shock before she was hit with another. "Just a moment. I'll get James."

"No, please. It's you I want to talk to."

"Me?"

"From your reaction, I'd guess James has mentioned me."

"Yes." Summer slumped down in a chair and closed her eyes. "You and James were engaged at one time."

"That's right. I understand you and James recently got married."

"Three months ago," Summer said, embarrassed by how weak her voice still was. "In Las Vegas," she added a little more loudly.

"I hope you'll forgive me for being so forward. I talked it over with Cody—he's my husband—and he said since I felt so strongly about it I should call you."

"So strongly about what?"

"About you . . . and James. I'll always regret the way I treated James. He deserved a lot better, but I was younger then. Immature in some ways. At one time I thought I was in love with him. I knew he loved me, and my family thought the world of him. Then I met Cody." She hesitated. "I didn't phone to tell you all this. I'm sure James filled in the details."

"Why did you call?" Summer was sure that under other circumstances she might have liked Christy Franklin.

"I wanted to tell you how happy I am that James found someone to love. I know it's presumptuous of me but I wanted to ask a favor of you."

"A favor?" The woman had a lot of nerve.

"Love him with all your heart, Summer. James is a special, special man and he deserves a woman who'll stand by his side and love him."

"I do," she said softly.

"For quite a while I despaired of James ever get-

191

ting married. I can't tell you how pleased I was when Mom phoned to tell me Rich and Jamie had met you. Cody and I want to extend our very best wishes to you both."

"Thank you."

"I know it's a lot to ask, but I do hope you'll keep Cody and me in mind when you count your friends. There's a place in my heart for James. He's been a friend to our family for years. He was a tremendous help to Paul when Diane died, and again later when he married Leah. James helped Rich and Jamie, too, and he's been a good friend to Jason and Charlotte, as well. We're all indebted to him one way or another."

"I do love him so much." She was fighting back tears and not even sure what she was crying about. The fact that Ralph Southworth had resigned as James's campaign manager because of her? Or that James's ex-fiancée still cared for him deeply?

Summer had just replaced the receiver when James stepped into the kitchen. He stood with one hand on the door.

"Who was that on the phone?" he asked.

Summer met his look straight on, waiting to read any emotion. "Christy Franklin."

"Christy?" he repeated. "What did she want?" He looked more surprised than anything.

"She called to give us her and Cody's best wishes. She said it was high time you were married and she can hardly wait to meet me."

"Really?"

"Really."

"And what did you tell her?"

Summer grinned. "I said she's to keep her cotton-pickin' hands off my husband."

James chuckled, obviously delighted by her possessive attitude. "You aren't going to get much of an argument from me."

"Good thing," she said, and slid her arm around his waist. Together they joined his father.

"I don't understand it," Summer muttered. She sucked in her stomach in order to close her skirt. "I can barely zip this up. It fit fine just last week."

"Honey, you're pregnant," James said matter-of-factly.

"Three months. I'm not supposed to show yet."

"You're not?" James's eyes left the mirror, his face covered with shaving cream. He carefully examined her rounded belly.

"Tell me the truth, James. If you were meeting me for the first time, would you guess I was pregnant?"

He frowned. "This isn't one of those trick questions, is it?"

"No."

"All right," he said, then cleared his throat. He seemed to know intuitively that she wasn't going to like the answer. "You do look pregnant to me.

But then you *are* pregnant, so I don't understand what the big deal is."

"I'm fat already," she wailed, and felt like breaking into tears.

"*Fat* is not the word I'd use to describe you."

"If I'm showing at three months, can you just imagine what I'll look like at nine?"

His grin revealed pride and love. "I'd say you'll look like the most beautiful woman in the world."

"No wonder I love you so much," she told her husband, turning back to the closet. She sorted through the hangers, dismissing first one outfit and then another.

"Where are you going that you're so worried about how you look?" James asked.

Summer froze. "An appointment." She prayed he wouldn't question her further. She'd arranged a meeting with Ralph Southworth, but she didn't want James to know about it.

"Okay. Don't forget tonight," he reminded her. "We're going to the Mannings' for dinner."

"I won't forget," she promised. "Eric and Elizabeth, right?"

"Right. Knowing Elizabeth, she'll probably spend the whole day cooking. She's called me at least five times in the past week. She's anxious to meet you."

"I'm anxious to meet them, too." But not nearly as anxious as she was about this meeting with Southworth. In setting up the appointment,

Summer hoped to achieve several objectives. Mainly she wanted Ralph to agree to manage James's campaign again. And she wanted to prove to James that he didn't need to protect her from gossip and speculation.

James left for court shortly after he'd finished shaving. Summer changed into the outfit she'd finally chosen, a soft gray business suit with a long jacket that—sort of—disguised her pregnancy. She spent the morning doing errands and arrived at Ralph's office at the Seattle Bank ten minutes ahead of their one-o'clock appointment.

She announced her name to the receptionist and was escorted into Southworth's office a few minutes later.

Ralph stood when she entered the room. He didn't seem pleased to see her.

"Hello again," she said brightly, taking the chair across from his desk. She wanted it understood that she wouldn't be easily dissuaded.

"Hello," he responded curtly.

"I hope you don't object to my making an appointment to see you. I'm afraid I may have, uh, misled your secretary into thinking it had to do with a loan."

"I see. Are you in the habit of misleading people?"

"Not at all," she assured him with a cordial smile, "but sometimes a little inventive thinking is worth a dozen frustrating phone calls."

Southworth didn't agree or disagree.

"I'll get to the point of my visit," she said, not wanting to waste time, his or hers.

"Please do."

"I'd like to know why you've resigned as my husband's campaign manager."

Southworth rolled a pencil between his palms, avoiding eye contact. "I believe that's between James and me. It has nothing to do with you."

"That isn't the way I understand it," she said, grateful he'd opened the conversation for her. "I overheard James and his father talking recently, and James said something different."

"So you eavesdrop, as well?"

He was certainly eager to tally her less than sterling characteristics.

"Yes, but in this case, I'm glad I did because I learned that you'd resigned because of me."

Southworth hesitated. "Not exactly. I questioned James's judgment."

"About our marriage?" she pressed.

Once again he seemed inclined to dodge the subject. "I don't really think . . ."

"I do, Mr. Southworth. This election is extremely important to James. *You're* extremely important to him. When he first mentioned your name to me, he said you were the best man for the job."

"I am the best man for the job." The banker certainly didn't lack confidence in his abilities. "I also know a losing battle when I see it."

"Why's that?"

"Mrs. Wilkens, please."

"Please what, Mr. Southworth? Tell me why you question James's judgment. Until he married me, you were ready to lend him your full support. I can assure you I'll stay right here until I have the answers to these questions." She raised her chin a stubborn half inch and refused to budge.

"If you insist . . ."

"I do."

"First, you're years younger than James."

"Nine years is hardly that much of a difference. This is a weak excuse and unworthy of you. I do happen to look young for my age, but I can assure you I'm twenty-eight, and James is only thirty-seven."

"There's also the fact that you're a showgirl."

"I'm an actress and singer," she countered. "Since I worked at Disneyland, I hardly think you can fault my morals."

"Morals is another issue entirely."

"Obviously," she said, finding she disliked this man more every time he opened his mouth. It seemed to her that Ralph Southworth was inventing excuses, none of which amounted to anything solid.

"You're pregnant."

"Yes. So?"

"So . . . it's clear to me, at least, that you and

James conveniently decided to marry when you recognized your condition."

Summer laughed. "That's not true, and even if it were, all I need to do is produce our marriage certificate, which I just happen to have with me." Somehow or other she knew it would come down to this. She opened her purse and removed the envelope, then handed it to the man whom her husband had once considered his friend.

Southworth read it over and returned it to her. "I don't understand why the two of you did this. No one meets in Vegas, falls in love and gets married within a few days. Not unless they've got something to hide."

"We're in love." She started to explain that she and James had known each other for a year, but Ralph cut her off.

"Please, Mrs. Wilkens! I've known James for at least a decade. There had to be a reason other than the one you're giving me."

"He loves me. Isn't that good enough for you?"

Southworth seemed bored with the conversation. "Then there's the fact that he kept the marriage a secret."

Summer had no answer to that. "I don't really know why James didn't tell anyone about the wedding," she admitted. "My guess is that it's because he's a private man and considers his personal life his own."

"How far along is the pregnancy?" he asked, ignoring her answer.

"Three months," she told him.

"Three months? I don't claim to know much about women and babies, but I've had quite a few women work for me at the bank over the years. A number of them have had babies. You look easily five or six months."

"That's ridiculous! I know when I got pregnant."

"Do you, now?"

Summer drew in her breath and held it for a moment in an effort to contain her outrage. She loved James and believed in him, but she refused to be insulted.

"I can see we aren't going to accomplish anything here," she said sadly. "You've already formed your opinion about James and me."

"About you, Mrs. Wilkens. It's unfortunate. James would've made an excellent superior court judge. But there's been far too much speculation about him lately. It started with the black eye. People don't want a man on the bench who can't hold on to his own temper. A judge should be above any hint of moral weakness."

"James is one of the most morally upright men I know," she said heatedly. "I take your comments as a personal insult to my husband."

"I find your loyalty to James touching, but it's too little, too late."

"What do you mean by that?" Summer demanded.

"You want your husband to win the election, don't you?"

"Yes. Of course." The question was ludicrous.

"If I were to tell you that you could make a difference, perhaps even sway the election, would you listen?"

"I'd listen," she said, although anything beyond listening was another matter.

Southworth stood and walked over to the window, which offered a panoramic view of the Seattle skyline. His back was to her and for several minutes he said nothing. He seemed to be weighing his words.

"You've already admitted I'm the best man to run James's campaign."

"Yes," she said reluctantly, not as willing to acknowledge it as she had been when she'd first arrived.

"I can help win him this September's primary and the November election. Don't discount the political sway I have in this community, Mrs. Wilkens."

Summer said nothing.

"When James first told me he'd married you, I suggested he keep you out of the picture until after the election."

"I see."

"I did this for a number of reasons, all of which James disregarded."

"He . . . he really didn't have much choice," she felt obliged to tell him. "I turned up on his doorstep, suitcase in hand."

Ralph nodded as if he'd suspected this had been the case. "I can turn James's campaign around if you'll agree to one thing."

Her stomach tightened, knowing before the words were out what he was going to say. "Yes?"

"Simply disappear for several months. Stay away from Seattle, and once the November election is over, you can move back into his house. It won't matter then."

She closed her eyes and lowered her head. "I see."

"Will you do it?"

"Summer, I'm sorry I'm late." James kissed her soundly and rushed up the stairs to change clothes.

He was late? She hadn't noticed. Since her meeting with Ralph Southworth, Summer had spent what remained of the afternoon in a stupor. She felt numb and sad. Tears lay just beneath the surface, ready to break free.

This decision should've been far less difficult. She could give her husband the dream he'd always wanted or ruin his life.

Five minutes later James was back. He'd changed out of his suit and tie and wore slacks and a shirt and sweater. "Are you ready?" he asked.

"For what?"

"Dinner tonight with the Mannings. Remember?"

"Of course," she said, forcing a smile. How could she have forgotten that? James was like a schoolboy eager to show off his science project. Only in this case, *she* was the project. She still wore her gray suit, so after quickly brushing her hair and refreshing her makeup, she considered herself ready—in appearance if not in attitude.

He escorted her out the front door and into his car, which he'd parked in front of the house. "You haven't had much campaigning to do lately," she commented.

"I know."

"What does Ralph have to say?" she asked, wanting to see how much James was willing to tell her.

"Not much. Let's not talk about the election tonight, okay?"

"Why not?"

"I don't want to have to think about it. These people are my friends. They're like a second set of parents to me."

"Do they know I'm pregnant?"

"No, but I won't need to tell them, will I?" He gently patted her abdomen.

"James," she whispered. "When we get home this evening, I want to make love."

His gaze briefly left the road and he nodded.

The emptiness inside her could only be filled with his love.

"Are you feeling all right?"

She made herself smile and laid her head against his shoulder. "Of course."

"There's something different about you."

"Is there?" Just that her heart felt as if it had been chopped in half. Just that she'd never felt so cold or alone in her life. Southworth had asked her to turn her back on the man she loved. He'd asked that she leave and do it in such a way that he wouldn't follow. He'd asked that she bear her child alone.

When they got to the Manning home, James parked his car on the street and turned to Summer. He studied her for an intense moment. "I love you."

"I love you," she whispered in return. She felt close to tears.

James helped her out of the car. They walked to the front porch, and he rang the doorbell. When she wasn't looking, he stole a kiss.

A distinguished older gentleman opened the door for them. "James! It's good to see you again."

"Eric, this is my wife, Summer."

"Hello, Summer." Instead of shaking her hand, Eric Manning hugged her.

They stepped inside, and all at once, from

behind every conceivable hiding space, people leapt out.

They were greeted with an unanimous chorus of "Surprise!"

Eleven

Summer didn't understand what was happening. A large number of strange people surrounded her. People with happy faces, people who seemed delighted to be meeting her.

"Elizabeth," James protested. "What have you done?"

The middle-aged woman hugged first James and then Summer. "You know how much I love a party," she told him, grinning broadly. "What better excuse than to meet your wife? I'm the mother of this brood," she told Summer proudly, gesturing around the room. There were men, women and children milling about. "You must be Summer."

"I am. You must be Elizabeth."

"Indeed I am."

Before she could protest, Summer was lured away from James's side. The men appeared eager to talk to James by himself. Summer looked longingly at her husband. He met her eyes, then shrugged and followed his friends into the family room.

Soon Summer found herself in the kitchen,

which bustled with activity. "I'm Jamie. We met the other day in the restaurant," Rich's wife reminded her.

"I remember," Summer told her, stepping aside as a youngster raced past her at breakneck speed.

"These two women with the curious looks on their faces are my sisters-in-law. The first one here," Jamie said, looping her arm around the woman who was obviously pregnant, "is Charlotte. She's married to Jason. He's the slob of the family."

"But he's improving," Charlotte told her.

"When's your baby due?"

"July," Charlotte said. "This is our second. Doug's asleep. I also have a daughter from my first marriage, but Carrie's working and couldn't be here. I'm sure you'll get a chance to meet her later."

"Our baby's due in September," Summer said, ending speculation.

The women exchanged glances. "You're just three months pregnant?"

Miserable, Summer nodded. "I think something must be wrong. The first couple of months I was really sick. I'm much better now that I'm in Seattle with James. But I'm ballooning. Hardly any of my clothes fit anymore."

"It happens like that sometimes," Elizabeth said with the voice of experience. "I wonder . . ." Then she shook her head. "I showed far more with Paul, my first, than I did with Christy, my youngest. Don't ask me why nature plays these silly tricks on us. You'd think we have enough to put up with, dealing with men."

A chorus of agreement broke out.

Elizabeth took the hors d'oeuvre platter out of the refrigerator. "The good news is I was blessed with three sons. The bad news is I was blessed with three sons." She laughed. "My daughters are an entirely different story."

"I don't know what to expect with this baby," Summer told everyone, pressing her hand to her stomach. "We didn't plan to get pregnant so soon."

"I'll bet James is thrilled."

Summer smiled and nodded. "We both are."

"This is Leah," Jamie said, introducing her other sister-in-law, who'd just entered the kitchen. "She's Paul's wife. Paul's the author in the family."

"He's very good," Leah said proudly. "His first book was published last year, and he's sold two more."

"That's great!"

"Let me help," Jamie insisted, removing the platter from Elizabeth's hands. She carried it to the long table, beautifully decorated with paper bells and a lovely ceramic bride-and-groom centerpiece.

"I've been waiting for a long time to use these

decorations," Elizabeth said disparagingly. "My children didn't give me the opportunity. It all started with the girls. Neither one of *them* saw fit to have a church wedding. Then Rich married Jamie and Paul married Leah, again without the kind of wedding I always wanted."

"Jason and Charlotte were the only ones to have a big wedding," Leah explained. "I don't think Eric and Elizabeth have ever forgiven the rest of us."

"You're darn right, we haven't," Eric said, joining them.

"They made it up to us with grandchildren, dear," his wife interjected. "Now, don't get started on that. We're very fortunate."

Summer couldn't remember the last time she'd sat down at a dinner table with this many people. A rowdy group of children ate at card tables set up in the kitchen. Twin boys seemed to instigate the chaos, taking delight in teasing their younger cousins. The noise level was considerable, but Summer didn't mind.

More than once, she caught James watching her. She smiled and silently conveyed that she was enjoying herself. Who wouldn't be?

There were gifts to open after the meal and plenty of marital advice. Summer, whose mood had been bleak earlier, found herself laughing so hard her sides ached.

The evening was an unqualified success, and

afterward Summer felt as if she'd met a houseful of new friends. Jamie, Leah and Charlotte seemed eager to make her feel welcome. Charlotte was the first to extend an invitation for lunch. Since they were both pregnant, they already had something important in common.

"A week from Friday," Charlotte reminded her as Summer and James prepared to leave. She mentioned the name of the restaurant and wrote her phone number on the back of a business card.

"I'll look forward to it," Summer told her and meant it.

It wasn't until they were home that she remembered her meeting with Southworth. She didn't know if she'd be in Seattle in another week, let alone available for lunch.

Sadness pressed against her heart.

James slipped his arm around her waist. He turned off the downstairs lights, and together they moved toward the stairs. "As I recall," he whispered in her ear, "you made me a promise earlier."

"I did?"

"You asked me to make love to you, remember?"

"Oh, yes . . ." Shivers of awareness slid up and down her spine.

"I certainly hope you intend to keep that promise."

She yawned loudly, covering her mouth, fighting back waves of tiredness. "I have no intention of changing my mind."

"Good." They reached the top of the stairs, and he nuzzled her neck. "I wonder if it'll always be like this," he murmured, steering her toward their bedroom.

"Like what?"

"My desire for you. I feel like a kid in a candy store."

Summer laughed, then yawned again. "I enjoyed meeting the Mannings. They're wonderful people."

"Are those yawns telling me something?" he asked.

She nodded. "I'm tired, James." But it was more than being physically weary. She felt a mental and emotional exhaustion that left her depleted.

"Come on, love," James urged gently. He led her into the bedroom and between long, deep kisses, he undressed her and placed her on the bed. He tucked her in and kissed her cheek.

The light dimmed, and Summer snuggled into the warmth. It took her a few minutes to realize James hadn't joined her.

"James?" She forced her eyes open.

"Yes, love?"

"Aren't you coming to bed?"

"Soon," he said. "I'm taking a shower first."

A shower, she mused, wondering at his sudden penchant for cleanliness.

Then she heard him mutter, "A nice, long, *cold* shower."

• • •

James had been looking forward to the ultrasound appointment for weeks. He'd met Dr. Wise, Summer's obstetrician, earlier and had immediately liked and trusted the man, who was in his late forties. David Wise had been delivering babies for more than twenty years, and his calm reassurance had gone a long way toward relieving James's fears.

The ultrasound clinic was in the same medical building as Dr. Wise's office. He'd said he'd join them there, although James wasn't convinced that was his regular policy. Still, he felt grateful.

Summer sat next to him in the waiting room, her face pale and lifeless. She hadn't been herself in the past few days, and James wondered what was bothering her. He didn't want to pry and hoped she'd soon share whatever it was.

They held hands and waited silently until Summer's name was called.

It was all James could do to sit still as the technician, a young woman named Rachel, explained the procedure.

Summer was instructed to lie flat on her back on the examining table. Her T-shirt was raised to expose the bump that was their child. As James smiled down on her Dr. Wise entered the room.

A gel was spread across Summer's abdomen. It must have been cold because she flinched.

"It's about this time that women start to suggest the male of the species should be responsible for childbearing," Dr. Wise told him.

"No, thanks," James said, "I like my role in all this just fine."

Dr. Wise chuckled. Rachel pressed a stethoscope-like instrument across Summer's stomach, and everyone's attention turned toward the monitor.

James squinted but had trouble making out the details on the screen.

"There's the baby's head," Dr. Wise said, pointing to a curved shape.

James squinted again and he noticed Summer doing the same.

"Well, well. Look at this," the physician continued. "I'm not altogether surprised."

"Look at what?" James studied the screen intently.

"We have a second little head."

"My baby has two heads?" Summer cried in alarm.

"Two heads?" James echoed.

"What I'm saying," Dr. Wise returned calmly, "is that there appear to be two babies."

"Twins?"

"It certainly seems that way." As the ultrasound technician moved the instrument across Summer's abdomen, Dr. Wise pointed to the monitor. "Here's the first head," he said, tracing the barely discernible round curve, "and here's the second."

James squinted for all he was worth just to see one. "Twins," he murmured.

"That explains a lot," Dr. Wise said, patting Summer's arm. "Let's run a copy of this for you both," he said, and Rachel pushed a series of buttons.

Within minutes they had the printout to examine for themselves. While Summer dressed, James studied the picture.

"Twins," he said again, just for the pleasure of hearing himself say it. He turned to Summer and smiled broadly. "Twins," he repeated, grinning from ear to ear.

She smiled, and James thought he saw tears in her eyes.

"It won't be so bad," he said, then immediately regretted his lack of sensitivity. He wasn't the one carrying two babies, nor would he be the one delivering them. "I'll do whatever I can to help," he quickly reassured her.

She gave him a watery smile.

"Say something," he pleaded. "Are you happy?"

"I don't know," she admitted. "I'm still in shock. What about you?"

"Other than the day I married you, I've never been happier." He couldn't seem to stop smiling. "I can hardly wait to tell my father. He's going to be absolutely thrilled."

Summer stared at the ultrasound. "Can you tell? Boys? Girls? One of each?" Strangely, perhaps, it hadn't occurred to her to ask Dr. Wise.

James scratched his head. "I had enough trouble finding the two heads. I decided not to try deciphering anything else."

They left the doctor's office and headed for the parking garage across the street.

"This calls for a celebration. I'll take you to lunch," he said.

"I was thinking more along the lines of a nap."

James grinned and looked at his watch. "Is there time?"

"James," she said, laughing softly. "I meant a *real* nap. I'm exhausted."

"Oh." Disappointment shot through him. "You don't want to celebrate with a fancy lunch?"

She shook her head. "Don't be upset with me. I guess I need time to think about everything."

That sounded odd to James. What was there to think about? True, Summer was pregnant with twins, but they had plenty of time to prepare. As for any mental readjustment, well, he'd made that in all of two seconds. The twins were a surprise, yes, but a pleasant one.

"This news has upset you, hasn't it?" he asked.

"No," she was quick to assure him. "It's just that . . . well, it changes things."

"What things?"

She shook her head again and didn't answer.

James frowned, not knowing how to calm her fears or allay her doubts. She didn't seem to expect him to do either and instead appeared to be withdrawing into herself.

"You don't mind if I tell my dad, do you?" he asked. If he didn't share the news with someone soon, he was afraid he'd be reduced to stopping strangers on the street.

She smiled at him, her eyes alight with love. "No, I don't mind if you tell Walter."

He walked her to where she'd parked and kissed her, then walked the short distance back to the King County Courthouse. His thoughts were so full of Summer that he went a block too far before he realized what he'd done.

In his office, the first thing he did was reach for the phone.

His father answered immediately. "You'll never guess what I'm looking at," he told Walter.

"You're right, I'll never guess."

"Today was Summer's ultrasound," James reminded him. Hiding his excitement was almost impossible.

"Ah, yes, and what did you learn?"

James could hear the eagerness in Walter's voice. "I have the picture in front of me."

"And?"

"I'm staring at your grandchildren right this second."

"Boy or girl?"

James couldn't help it. He laughed. "You didn't listen very well."

"I did, too, and I want to know—what do we have? A boy or a girl?"

"Could be one of each," James informed him calmly.

"Twins!" Walter shouted. "You mean Summer's having twins?"

"That's what I'm telling you."

"Well, I'll be! This is good news. No, it's great news. The best!"

James had never heard Walter this excited—practically as excited as he was himself.

It wasn't every day that a man learned he was having not one baby but two!

Summer didn't go directly home. Instead, she drove around for at least an hour, evaluating the situation between her and James. She loved him so much. The thought of leaving him, even when she knew it was the best thing for his career, brought her to the verge of tears.

What she wanted was to talk with her mother, but her parents were vacationing, touring the south in their motor home. They weren't due back for another month. Summer received postcards every few days with the latest updates and many exhortations to look after herself and their unborn grandchild. Wait till she told them it was grand-*children,* she thought with a brief smile.

This vacation was good for them, but she really needed her mother now.

Without realizing she knew the way, Summer drove to the Manning family home. She parked, wondering whether she was doing the right thing.

It took her a full five minutes to gather up enough nerve to get out of the car, walk up the steps and ring the bell.

Elizabeth Manning answered the door. Her face lit up with warmth. "Summer! What a lovely surprise."

"I hope I haven't come at an inconvenient time."

"Not at all," Elizabeth said, ushering her in. "I was making meatballs. It's Eric's favorite. Today's his bowling day, so he's out just now. Can I get you a cup of tea?"

"No, thank you."

Elizabeth sat down in the living room.

"Would it be all right if we talked in the kitchen?" Summer asked after an awkward moment.

"Of course."

"I . . . I'm aware that you barely know me, and it's an imposition for me to drop in like this."

"Not at all. I'm delighted to see you again."

"I . . . my parents have a motor home," Summer said, wishing now she'd thought this through more carefully before she approached James's friends. "They're traveling across the south."

216

"Eric and I do quite a bit of traveling in our own motor home. We visit Christy and her sister, Taylor, at least once a year. Montana's become like a second home to us." She dug her hands into the bowl of hamburger and removed a glob of meat. Expertly she formed it into a perfect round shape.

"I really just wanted to thank you for everything you did the other night," Summer said. "The party for James and me . . ."

She suddenly decided she couldn't burden this woman with her troubles. She would've welcomed advice, but felt uncomfortable discussing her problems with someone who was little more than a stranger to her.

"When you know me better," Elizabeth was saying, "you'll learn that I love throwing parties. James has always been a special friend to our family, and we were so happy to find out about his marriage. Naturally we wanted to celebrate."

Summer nodded. "I didn't think it was possible to love anyone so much," she confessed, and then because tears began to drip from her eyes, she stood abruptly. "Listen, I should go, but thank you. I'll see myself to the door."

"Summer," Elizabeth called after her. "Summer, is everything all right?"

Summer was in her car by the time Elizabeth appeared in the doorway. She hurriedly started the engine and drove off, sure that she'd done more harm than good with her impromptu visit.

Wiping away tears, Summer went home. She walked into the house and up the stairs, then lay down on the bed and closed her eyes.

She had to leave, but she didn't know where to go. If she didn't do it soon, she'd never find the courage. Only minutes earlier, she'd declared to James's family friend how deeply she loved her husband. That was the truth, so doing what was best for him shouldn't be this difficult.

But it was.

Sobbing and miserable, Summer got up from the bed and pulled a big suitcase from the closet. She packed what she thought she'd need and carried it down to the car.

At the last minute she decided she couldn't leave without writing James. She sat at his desk for several minutes, trying to compose a letter that would explain what she was doing and why. But it was all so complicated, and in the end she simply said he was better off without her and signed her name. She read it twice before tucking it in an envelope.

Tears streamed down her cheeks. It wouldn't be so bad, or so she attempted to convince herself. The babies would be less than two months old when the election was over, and then she'd be free to return.

If James wanted her back.

James had seldom been in a better mood. He sat in the courtroom, convinced he must be grinning like a fool.

His assistant didn't know what to think. During a brief recess, he waltzed back to his office to phone Summer, whistling as he went.

His wife might not have wanted to celebrate with lunch, but their news deserved some kind of festivity. Dinner at the Space Needle. A night on the town.

While he was in his office, he ordered flowers for Summer with a card that said she'd made him the happiest man alive. Twice. He wondered what the florist would make of *that.*

The phone rang four times before voice mail kicked in. James hung up rather than leave a message. He'd try again later. Summer was probably resting; he hoped the phone hadn't disturbed her.

"Judge Wilkens?" Mrs. Jamison, his assistant, stopped him as he was leaving his office.

"Yes?"

"Your father phoned earlier. He wanted me to let you know he's been to the toy store and purchased two giant teddy bears. He also asked me to tell you he'll be dropping them off around six this evening. And he said he made dinner reservations in case you hadn't thought of it."

"Great." James laughed and discovered his assistant staring at him blankly.

"See this," James said, taking the ultrasound picture from inside his suit pocket. "My wife and I just learned we're having twins."

"Your wife? Twins for you and Summer. Why, Your Honor . . ." Her mouth opened, then shut, but she recovered quickly. "Congratulations!"

"Thank you," James said. Then, checking his watch, he returned to the courtroom.

The afternoon was hectic. James was hearing the sad case of a man who, crazed with drugs and alcohol, had gone on a shooting rampage. He'd killed three people and injured seventeen more. The case was just getting underway but was sure to attract a lot of media attention. James knew the defense was hinging its case on a plea of temporary insanity.

A door opened at the rear of the courtroom. James didn't look up, but out of the corner of his eye, he saw a lone figure slip into the back row. Whoever it was apparently didn't want to be recognized. She wore a scarf and large sunglasses.

Twice more James found his gaze returning to the figure in the back of the courtroom. If he didn't know better, he'd think it was Summer.

Whoever it was stayed for quite a long time. An hour or more. He wasn't sure when the woman left, but James couldn't help being curious.

His best guess was that the woman was a reporter.

When he was finished for the afternoon, James

returned to his office and removed his robe. His secretary brought in a stack of phone messages. The one that seemed most peculiar was from Elizabeth Manning. She'd never called him at court.

Leaning back in his chair, he reached for the phone. "Hello, Elizabeth," he said cheerfully. It was on the tip of his tongue to tell her his and Summer's good news, but she cut him off.

"You'd better tell me what's wrong. I've been worried sick all afternoon."

"Worried? About what?"

"You and Summer."

Sometimes she baffled him. "I don't have a clue what you're talking about. I will tell you that Summer and I were at the doctor's this morning and found out she's pregnant with twins."

"Congratulations." But Elizabeth seemed distracted. "That can't be it," she mulled aloud. "She was here, you know."

"Who?"

"Summer."

"When?"

"This afternoon. Listen to me, James, there's something wrong. I knew it the minute I saw that girl. She was upset and close to tears. At first I thought you two might've had an argument."

"No . . ." James frowned. "What did she say?"

"She talked about her parents traveling in their motor home. I suppose I should've realized she wanted to discuss something with me, but I started chattering, hoping she'd relax enough to speak her mind."

"Tell me everything that happened."

"After the part about her parents' vacation, she said she'd come to thank me for the party, which we both knew was an excuse. Then she apparently changed her mind about talking with me and started to cry. Before I could stop her, she was gone."

"Gone? What do you mean gone?"

"The girl literally ran out of the house. I tried to catch up with her, but with my bad leg, that was impossible."

"She drove off without another word?"

"That's right." Elizabeth sounded flustered. "What could be wrong, James?"

"I don't know. I just don't know. She was fine this morning." Or was she? James had no idea anymore. "I'll give you a call this evening," he assured Elizabeth. "I'm sure everything's okay."

"I hope so. Summer was very upset, James. Oh. That's odd. . . ."

"What is?"

"I remember something else she said, and it was after this that she started to cry."

"What was it?" James asked anxiously.

"She told me how much she loved you."

A few minutes later, when he'd finished speaking to Elizabeth, James was more confused than ever. He tried calling Summer again—but again there was no answer. He left the office abruptly, without a word to his staff.

When he got to the house he burst through the front door. "Summer!" he shouted, his heart racing.

He was greeted with silence.

He raced up the stairs, taking them two at a time. He searched every room but couldn't find her.

What confused him further was that her clothes still hung in her closet, but one suitcase was missing. Surely if she was planning to leave him, she'd have taken more things. The only items that seemed to be missing were her toothbrush, slippers and a book about pregnancy and birth.

Baffled, he wandered back downstairs. He scouted out the kitchen and the other rooms. The last place he looked was in his den. There he found an envelope propped against the base of the lamp.

James tore open the letter. It was brief and it made no sense. All he understood was that she'd left him. He had no idea why, other than that she seemed to think she was doing what was best for him.

He immediately called her cell. No answer.

A sick feeling attacked his stomach. He sat numbly at his desk for what could've been minutes or hours; he'd lost track of time. The next thing he knew, the doorbell chimed. He didn't get up to answer. A moment later the door opened on its own and his father came into the house.

"You might've let me in," he grumbled, setting one huge teddy bear in the chair across from James. "I'll be right back." He returned a couple of minutes later with the second bear.

"How'd you get in?" James asked, his voice devoid of emotion.

"You gave me a key, remember?"

He didn't.

"What's going on around here?" Walter asked. "Where's my daughter-in-law who's giving me twin grandkids?"

"Apparently Summer has decided to leave me. She's gone."

Twelve

"Gone?" Walter protested. "What do you mean, gone?"

"Gone, Dad," James said bitterly, "as in packed-a-suitcase-and-walked-out-the-door gone."

His father quickly sat down. "But . . . why?"

James couldn't answer that; silently he handed Walter the brief letter Summer had left him.

Walter read it, then raised questioning eyes to James. "What's this supposed to mean?"

"Your guess is as good as mine."

"You must've said something," Walter insisted. "Think, boy, think."

"I've done nothing *but* think, and none of this makes sense. I thought at first that she was upset about the twins. I realize now that whatever it is has been worrying her for some time."

"What could it be?"

"I don't know. I'd hoped she'd tell me."

"You mean to say you didn't ask?"

"No."

Walter glared at him in disbelief. "That's the first thing I learned after I married your mother. She never told me a thing that I didn't have to pry out of her with a crowbar. It's a man's duty, a husband's lot in life. When you didn't ask, Summer must've assumed you didn't care. She probably figures you don't love her."

In spite of his heavy heart, James smiled. "Trust me, Dad, Summer has no fear of speaking her mind, and as for my loving her, she couldn't have doubted that for an instant."

"She loves you." Walter's words were more statement than question.

"Yes," James said. He felt secure in her love. Or he had until now.

"Where would she go?"

This was the same question he'd been debating from the moment he discovered her letter. He shrugged. "No idea."

"Have you tried her cell?"

"Of course," he snapped. "She turned it off."

"Did you contact her parents?"

He would have, but it wouldn't help. James rubbed his face, tired to the very marrow of his bones. "They're traveling across the Southwest in their motor home. Half the time they don't have cell phone coverage."

"What about friends she's made since the move?"

"They're more acquaintances than friends. She's planning to volunteer at the library, but she's only mentioned the children's librarian in passing."

"I see." Walter frowned. "What about the Mannings?"

"She went over to talk to Elizabeth earlier this afternoon. Elizabeth phoned me and said Summer started to cry and then left in a hurry."

Walter's look was thoughtful. "Sounds as if she was trying to reach out for help."

"The only other person I can think of is her former roommate, Julie. I'll call her now."

"Julie, of course," his father said as if he should've thought of her himself.

James looked up the number and spoke to Julie's new roommate for several minutes.

"Julie's contract with Disney was up at the same time as Summer's," he said as he hung up. "Now that I think about it, Summer did say something about Julie being on tour with a musical group."

"So she'd be staying in hotels. Unlikely Summer would go to her."

James closed his eyes. His wife had walked out on him into a cold, friendless world.

"What about her brother?"

After another quick call, James shook his head. "Adam and Denise haven't heard from her. All I did was scare them," he said grimly.

"Did you check the airlines?"

"Where would she go?" James asked, losing his patience.

"I don't know," Walter admitted reluctantly. He began pacing.

His movements soon irritated James. "For heaven's sake, will you kindly sit down?"

"I can't sit here and do nothing."

"Yes, you can and you will," James insisted, making a decision. "I'll take the car and drive around, see if I can find her. You stay here by the phone in case she calls or we hear something."

"Okay. Check in with me every half hour."

James nodded. As he climbed into the car, he felt as if he was setting out on a journey without a map. Essentially he was, he thought as he drove through the narrow neighborhood streets. Try as he might, he couldn't figure out where she'd go. He tried to put himself in her shoes. Alone in a strange city with few friends.

The only thing he could do was ask God to guide him.

The wind blew off Puget Sound and buffeted Summer as she stood at the end of the pier. The waterfront was one of her favorite places in all of Seattle. Not knowing where else to instruct the taxi to take her, she'd had the driver bring her here.

She loved to shop at the Pike Place Market. Every Saturday morning James came down to the waterfront with her, and they bought fresh fruit and vegetables for the week. He'd been wonderfully patient while she browsed in the tourist shops that stretched along the waterfront. Some of their happiest moments in Seattle had been spent on this very pier.

How she hated to leave this city. It was as if everything in her was fighting to keep her in Seattle. Her husband was here, her home, her very life.

The instant she'd walked into James's large house, she'd experienced a powerful sense of homecoming. She'd never said anything to her husband—he might think her reaction was silly— but Summer felt that his house had always been meant for them together.

She'd like to think that somewhere in James's subconscious he'd known he was going to fall in love and marry. The house had been his preparation for her entry into his life.

Tears blinded her eyes. She didn't want to focus on her unhappiness, so she turned her attention to the water. The pull of the tide fascinated her. The dark, murky waters of Elliott Bay glistened in the lights overhead. A green-and-white ferry chugged into the terminal.

Summer closed her eyes, willing herself to walk away. Except that she didn't know where she'd go. One thing was certain; she couldn't spend the night standing at the end of the pier. She'd need to find herself a hotel. In the morning her head would be clearer and she could make some decisions.

She was about to reach for her suitcase when she sensed someone approaching. Not wanting company, even the nonintrusive sort, Summer turned away from the railing. She kept her eyes lowered, but that didn't prevent her from recognizing James.

He sauntered to the railing several feet from where she stood. Wordlessly he stared into the distance.

Summer wasn't sure what she should do. She couldn't very well walk away from him now. It had been difficult enough the first time. She didn't have the strength to do it again.

"How'd . . . how'd you find me?" she asked.

He continued to stare into the distance. "Lucky guess," he finally said in cool tones.

Summer doubted that James felt lucky being married to her just then. He was furious with her. More furious than she'd ever seen him.

She wanted to explain that she was a detriment to his career, but couldn't force the words through her parched throat.

The tears that had flowed most of the day returned. She brushed them away with her fingertips.

"Was I such a bad husband?" he demanded in the same chilling tone.

"No," she whispered.

"Did I do something so terrible you can't forgive me for?"

Sobbing, she shook her head.

"You've fallen out of love with me," he suggested next.

"Don't be ridiculous," she cried. If she'd loved him any more than she already did, her heart couldn't have stood it.

"Then tell me why you walked out on me."

"My letter . . ."

". . . explained nothing."

"I . . . I . . ." She was trembling so much she couldn't speak.

James walked over to her and reached for her suitcase. "We're going back to the house and we're going to talk about this. Then, if you're still set on leaving, I'll drive you to the airport myself. Understand?"

All she could manage was a weak nod.

Thankfully, he'd parked the car close by. Summer felt disoriented. Maybe she shouldn't be this happy that James had found her, but she was. Even if he was angry with her, she was grateful he was taking her home.

James opened the car door for her and set her suitcase in the backseat. He didn't speak so much as a single word on the drive home.

When they pulled into the driveway, Summer saw Walter's car.

"Your father's here?"

James didn't answer her. Nor did he need to. Walter was already out the door.

"Where'd you find her?" he asked, bolting toward them.

"The waterfront."

"Sit down, sit down," her father-in-law murmured, guiding Summer inside and into a chair. She felt she was about to collapse and must have looked it, too.

"Now what the hell is this all about?" James said roughly.

"You can't talk to her like that," Walter chastised. "Can't you see the poor girl's had the worst day of her life?" He turned to Summer, smiling gently. "Now what the hell is this all about?"

Summer looked from one man to the other. "Would it be all right if I spoke to James alone?" she asked her father-in-law. She couldn't deal with both of them at the same time.

It looked for a moment as if Walter wasn't going to leave. "I suppose," he agreed with reluctance. "I'll be in the other room."

"Walter," Summer said, stopping him on his

way out the door. "I take it the two teddy bears are your doing."

He nodded sheepishly. "The car's loaded with goodies. I'm afraid I got a little carried away."

"These babies are going to love their grandpa."

Walter grinned, then walked out, closing the door.

James stood by the fireplace, his back to her. Summer suspected he was preparing a list of questions. She wasn't even sure she had all the answers; she wasn't sure she wanted him to ask them. She decided to preempt his interrogation.

"I . . . I went to see Ralph Southworth," she said in a quavering voice.

James whirled around. "You did *what?*"

"I . . . I overheard you and your father talking not long ago and I learned that Southworth resigned as your campaign manager."

"So he's what this is all about," James said thoughtfully. His eyes hardened. "What happened between the two of us had nothing to do with you."

"James, please, I know otherwise. I . . . I knew from the start that Ralph disapproved of me. I'm not sure why, but it doesn't matter."

"No, it doesn't. Because Southworth doesn't matter."

Summer didn't believe that. "Afterward, it seemed like you'd given up on the election. In the last two weeks you haven't made a single public appearance. When I ask, you don't want to talk about it and—"

"There are things you don't know."

"Things you wouldn't tell me."

James sat across from her and leaned forward, elbows on his knees. He didn't say anything for several minutes.

"What was I supposed to think?" she cried when he didn't explain. "Being a judge is the most important thing in the world to you. You were born for this. . . . I couldn't take it away from you. Don't you understand?"

"You're wrong about something. Being a superior court judge means nothing if you're not with me. I guarantee you, my career's not worth losing my wife and family over."

"I was going to come back," she whispered, her eyes lowered. "After the election . . ."

"Do you mean to say you were going to deliver our babies on your own? Do you honestly think I wouldn't have turned this city upside down looking for you?"

"I . . . didn't know what to think. Ralph said—"

"Don't even tell me." A muscle leapt in his jaw. "I can well imagine what he said. The man's a world-class idiot. He saw you as a liability when you're my greatest asset."

"If you truly believe that, then why did you throw in the towel?"

"I haven't," he told her. "I took a few days to

think about it and decide who I'll ask to manage the rest of my campaign. It seems there are several people who want the job."

"But Southworth said he could sway the election for you. . . . He claims to have political clout."

"He seems to think he does," James said tightly.

"We made a deal," she whispered, lowering her gaze.

"What kind of deal?"

"Southworth agreed to manage your campaign if I left Seattle until after the election."

James snickered. "It's unfortunate you didn't check with me first."

"Why?"

"I don't want Southworth anywhere near my campaign."

Summer bristled. "You might've said that earlier."

"True," James admitted slowly. "But I wanted everything squared away before I announced that I'd changed campaign managers."

"So, who did you choose? Who's your new manager?"

"Eric Manning. He's not only an old friend, he was a successful businessman and he's very well connected." He shook his head. "I should've asked him in the first place."

"James, that's wonderful! I like him so much better than Ralph."

James reached for her hands and held them in

his own. "What you don't understand is that I wouldn't have taken Southworth back under any circumstances. First of all, I won't allow any man to talk about my wife the way he did. It's true I made some mistakes when we first got married. I blame myself for not publishing our wedding announcement immediately. Frankly, I didn't think of it."

"I didn't, either. And remember, we were talking about an April ceremony back then." Summer wasn't willing to have him accept all the blame.

"You're my wife, and I couldn't be prouder that someone as beautiful and talented as you would choose to marry me. Ralph made it sound as if we should keep you under wraps until after the election, which is utterly ridiculous. I'm angry with myself for not taking a stand sooner."

"What about the election?" She didn't care to hear any more about Southworth.

"I'll get to that in a minute. When Southworth said he questioned my judgment, I realized what a fool I'd been to listen to the man for even a minute."

"But—"

"Let me finish, sweetheart. The best thing I ever did in my life was marry you."

"It was impulsive and—"

"Smart," he said, cutting her off. "I don't need Southworth to win this campaign for me. He had me convinced I did, but I know otherwise now."

"What about his political friends?"

"That's a laugh. A man as narrow-minded and self-righteous as Ralph Southworth can't afford the luxury of friends. He has none, but he doesn't seem to know it. If he hadn't decided to leave my campaign, I would've asked him to resign."

It was a good thing Summer was sitting down. "You mean to say I went through all that grief and left you for *nothing?*"

"Exactly."

"Oh."

James gathered her in his arms. "Summer, whatever I am, whatever I may become, I'm nothing without you."

Summer sobbed into his shoulder.

"Winning the election would be an empty victory if you weren't standing at my side. I want you to share that moment with me. I love you, Summer, and I love our babies, too."

"Oh, James, I've been so unhappy. I didn't know what to do."

"Don't ever leave me again. It was like I'd lost my mind, my heart—everything—until I saw you standing at the end of that pier."

Summer tightened her arms around him.

Walter tapped on the door. "Can I come in yet?"

"No," James growled.

"So have you two settled your differences?"

"We're working on it," Summer called out.

"Then I'll leave you to your reunion."

"Good night, Dad," James said in what was an obvious hint for his father to leave.

"'Night, kids. Kiss and make up, okay?"

"We're going to do a lot more than kiss," James whispered in her ear.

"Promises, promises, promises," she murmured.

"You can bet I'll make good on these."

Thirteen

"This is my wife, Summer," James said, his arm around her thick waist. Although she was only six months pregnant, she looked closer to nine.

"I'm so pleased to meet you," the older woman said.

"Who was that again?" she whispered to James.

"Emily Rohrbaugh, president of the League of Women Voters."

"Oh. I don't know how you remember all these names. I'm impressed."

"I'm more impressed that you can remember all your lines in *Beauty and the Beast*," he said. "But here's my little trick for recalling names. I try to tie them in with something else," James told her. "Some kind of object or action."

"Rohrbaugh is something of a challenge, don't you think?" Summer raised her eyebrows.

"Roar and baa," he said under his breath. "Think of a lion and a lamb. A lion roars and a lamb goes *baa*. Rohrbaugh."

Summer's face lit up with a bright smile. "No wonder I married you. You're brilliant."

"I bet you won't have a problem remembering Emily the next time you meet."

"I won't."

"She's a good friend of Elizabeth Manning's," James said, feeding his wife a seedless grape. It was a test of his restraint not to kiss her afterward. One would assume his desire for her would fade after all these months; if anything, quite the opposite had occurred. She was never more beautiful to him than now, heavy with their children.

"Elizabeth Manning?" Summer repeated. "I didn't think she'd be the political type."

"She isn't," James said. They mingled with the crowd gathered on the patio of an influential member of the state senate. "But the two of them have been friends since high school."

"I see."

"Do you need to sit for a while?"

"James," she groaned. "Stop worrying about me."

He glanced down at her abdomen. "How are Mutt and Jeff?"

She circled her belly with both hands. "I swear these two are going to be world-class soccer players."

James chuckled, reaching for an hors d'oeuvre from one of the several platters set around the sunny patio. He gave it to Summer.

"James, I don't believe I've met your wife."

James recognized the voice—William Carr, the president of the Bar Association. He quickly made the introductions. He never worried about Summer saying the wrong thing or inadvertently embarrassing him. She had a natural way about her that instantly put people at ease. She was charming and open and genuine. These political functions weren't her idea of a good time, but she never complained. She seemed eager to do whatever she could to aid his campaign and had proved to be the asset he knew she would be.

"I'm very pleased to meet you," she said warmly as they exchanged handshakes.

The obvious topic of conversation was Summer's pregnancy, which they discussed but only briefly. She managed to deftly turn the conversation away from herself, and soon Carr was talking about himself, laughing over the early days when his wife was pregnant with their oldest child.

After ten minutes or so, Summer excused herself.

"She's an excellent conversationalist," William Carr commented as she walked away.

James did his best to hide a smile. It amused him that Carr could do most of the talking and then act as if Summer had been the one carrying the discussion.

"It seems strange to think of you as married," the attorney said next.

"When I'm with Summer, I wonder why I ever waited so long."

Carr shifted his weight from one foot to the other. "If I'd given you advice before you were appointed to the court, it would've been to marry."

"Really?" This came as a shock to James.

"You're a fine young man, and I expect great things from you. Just between you, me and the fence post, I think you're doing an excellent job."

"I hope so," James said, but there were some who weren't as confident as William Carr. Generally those under the influence of Ralph Southworth. To James's surprise, Southworth had managed to prejudice several supporters against him.

"You remind me of myself thirty years back," Carr told him.

James considered this high praise. "Thank you."

"But you needed a little softening around the edges. You came off as strong and unbending. Not a bad thing for a judge, mind you, but being a little more human wouldn't have hurt."

"I see." James didn't like hearing this but knew it was for his own good, however uncomfortable it might be.

"It's easy to sit in judgment of others when you live in an ivory tower."

James frowned uncertainly. "I don't understand."

"Until you married Summer, your life was a bit . . . sterile. Protected. If you don't mind my saying so . . . A married man knows how to compromise. I imagine you've done things to make your wife happy that you wouldn't normally do."

He nodded.

"In my opinion, marriage matures a man. It helps him sympathize and identify with his fellow humans."

"Are you trying to tell me I was a stodgy stuffed shirt before I married Summer?" James asked outright.

William Carr seemed taken aback by his directness, then grinned. "Couldn't have said it better myself."

"That's what I thought." James reached for a tiny crab puff.

"By the way, I wanted to congratulate you on a job well done. That multiple homicide was your first murder trial, wasn't it?"

"Yes." To be honest, he was happy it was over. The ordeal had proved to be exhausting for everyone involved. The jury had found the young man guilty, and after careful deliberation, James had pronounced the sentence.

His name and face had appeared on television screens every night for weeks. It went without saying that a lot of people were watching and waiting to see how he'd rule. Liberals were looking for leniency, and hard-liners wanted the death penalty. James had agonized over the sentence.

There were more victims than the ones who were shot during those hours of madness. Three families had lost loved ones. Seventeen others would always carry the mark of a madman's gun. Innocent lives had been forever changed.

James had delivered a sentence he felt was fair. He didn't try to satisfy any political factions, although the outcome of the election could well rest on his judgment. He'd sentenced the killer to life without the possibility of parole, with mandatory psychiatric treatment.

It would've been impossible to keep everyone happy, so his decision had been based on what he considered equitable for all concerned. Some were pleased, he knew, and others were outraged.

"Thank you," James said, "I appreciate your vote of confidence."

"The decisions won't get any easier," William Carr told him. The older man grabbed a stuffed green olive and popped it in his mouth.

"The bar will be taking their opinion poll about the time your wife's due to have those babies of yours."

James knew that whether or not the results were published was at the discretion of the bar. The vote could sway the November election.

Summer returned just then, looking tired. Despite her smile, William Carr seemed to realize this. He wished them his best and drifted away.

"Are you ready to leave?" James asked.

"No," she protested. "We've barely arrived."

"We're going." His mistake was in asking her; he should've known to expect an argument.

He made their excuses, thanked the host and hostess and urged Summer toward their parked car. Her progress was slow, and he knew she was uncomfortable, especially in the heat.

"Charlotte's due in two weeks," she said when he helped her inside. She sighed as she eased into the seat. The seat belt barely stretched all the way around her.

James paused. "What's that comment about Charlotte about?"

"I envy her. Look at me, James!"

"I am looking at you," he said, and planted a kiss on her cheek. "You're the most beautiful woman in the world."

"I don't believe you," she muttered.

"You'd better, because it wouldn't take much to convince me to prove it right here and now."

"James, honestly."

"I am being honest."

She smiled, and he couldn't resist kissing her a second time.

After they got home, Summer sat outside in the

sunshine. She propped her feet on a stool, and her hands rested on her stomach.

James brought her a glass of iced tea.

She smiled her appreciation. "You spoil me."

"That's because I enjoy it." He sat down next to her. "I don't suppose you've thought about packing up and leaving me lately?"

Summer giggled. "Once or twice, but by the time I finished dragging out my suitcases, I was too tired to go."

"You're teasing."

"Of course I'm teasing."

"Speaking of suitcases, do you have one ready for the hospital?"

"Aren't we being a little premature?"

"Who knows what Mutt and Jeff are thinking." James's hand joined hers. It thrilled him to feel his children move inside her. "And this time you might want to take more than your toothbrush, a book and your bedroom slippers."

"That goes to show you the mental state I was in."

"Never again," James said firmly.

Summer propped her head against his shoulder and sighed. "Never again," she agreed.

The day of the September primary, Summer woke feeling sluggish and out of sorts. Getting out of bed was a task of monumental proportions. She felt as if she needed a forklift.

James was already up and shaved. He'd been watching her carefully all week. To everyone's surprise, including her doctor's, Summer hadn't delivered the twins yet. She'd read that twins were often born early. But not Mutt and Jeff, as they'd been affectionately named by James.

"Most babies aren't born on their due dates, so stop looking so worried. This is *your* day." She sat on the edge of the bed and pressed her hand to the small of her back.

James offered her his arm to help her upright. "How do you feel?"

"I don't know yet." The pain at the base of her spine had kept her awake most of the night. It didn't seem to go away, no matter how often she changed her position.

"When are we voting?" she asked.

"First thing this morning," James told her.

"Good."

"Why is that good?" he asked anxiously. "Do you think today's the day?"

"James, stop! I'm in perfect health."

"For someone nine months pregnant with twins, you mean."

Summer swore that somehow, God willing, she'd make it through this day. James was so tender and endearing, but she didn't want him worrying about her during the primary.

They gathered, together with Walter, at the large Manning home for the election results that evening. Summer was pleased for the opportunity to be with her friends.

Jason and Charlotte, along with their toddler and infant daughter, Ann Marie, were among the first to arrive. Many of the friends who'd worked so hard on James's campaign showed up soon after, shortly before the first election results were announced.

Summer planted herself in a chair in the family room and didn't move for an hour. The ache in her back had intensified.

Feeling the need to move about, she made her way into the kitchen. She was standing in front of the sink when it happened. Her eyes widened as she felt a sharp, stabbing pain.

"James," she cried in panic, gripping the counter. Water gushed from between her legs and onto the floor. "Oh, my goodness."

"Summer?" James stood in the doorway, along with at least ten others, including Elizabeth Manning.

"I'm sorry," she whispered, looking at James. "But I think it might be time to take me to the hospital."

She saw her husband turn and stare longingly at the election results being flashed across the screen. "Now?"

Fourteen

"James . . . I'm sorry." The pain that had been concentrated in the small of her back had worked its way around her middle. Summer held her stomach and closed her eyes, surprised by the intensity of it.

"Sorry," James demanded, "for what?" He moved quickly and placed his arm around her shoulders.

"You'd better get her to the hospital," Elizabeth advised.

"I'll phone the doctor for you," Eric added.

James shouted out the number he'd memorized, and five or six Mannings chanted it until Eric found a pad and pen to write it down.

Summer felt as if everyone wanted to play a role in the birth of their twins.

"Toss me the car keys, and I'll get the car as close to the front door as I can," Jason Manning shouted.

James threw him the keys, and Jason hurried out the front door.

"What about the election returns?" Summer asked, gazing at the television.

"I'll get them later," James said as if it meant nothing.

"I'll leave messages on your cell phone," Charlotte volunteered, "and James can call us when he has an update on Summer and the babies."

Summer bit her lip at the approach of another contraction. It hurt, really hurt. "James." She squeezed his hand, needing him.

"I'm here, sweetheart. I won't leave you, not for anything."

Jason reappeared, and the small entourage headed for James's car. It was parked on the grass, close to the front door, the engine running.

"The doctor said you should go directly to the hospital," Walter said breathlessly. "He'll meet you there."

"Don't worry, Summer, this isn't his first set of twins," Elizabeth said in a reassuring voice.

"True, but they're mine," James said.

"James?" Summer looked at her husband and noticed how pale he'd suddenly become. "Are you all right?"

He didn't answer for a moment; instead, he helped her inside the car and strapped her in. Before long he was sitting next to her, hands braced on the steering wheel. Summer saw the pulse in his neck pounding.

"It's going to be fine," she whispered. "Just fine."

"I'll feel a whole lot better once we get you to the hospital."

"Call us," Charlotte shouted, standing on the steps, waving.

Summer waved back, and no fewer than fifteen adults crowded onto the Mannings' front porch, cheering them on.

"James, are you okay to drive?" Summer asked when he took off at breakneck speed. He slowed down and stayed within the speed limit, but there was a leashed fear in him that was almost palpable.

"I'll be okay once we get you to the hospital."

"The birthing process is perfectly natural."

"Maybe it is for a woman, but it isn't as easy for a man."

With her hands propped against her abdomen, Summer smiled. "What's that supposed to mean?"

"I don't know if I can bear to see you in pain," he said, wiping his face as they stopped for a red light.

"It won't be too bad."

"Hey, you saw the films in our birthing class. I don't know if I'm ready for this."

"You!" she said, and giggled.

James's fingers curled around her hand. "This isn't a laughing matter. I've never been more frightened in my life. No, only once," he amended. "The night I came home and found you gone."

"The babies and I are going to be just fine," she said again. "Don't worry, James, please. This is your night to shine. I'm just sorry Mutt and Jeff chose right now to make their debut."

"At the moment, the election is the last thing on my mind. None of it matters."

"You're going to win the primary," she insisted. Summer knew the competition had been steep, and Ralph Southworth had done what damage he could, eager to prove himself right.

"We're almost at the hospital," James said, sounding relieved.

"Relax," she said, and as it turned out, her words were a reminder to herself. The next contraction hit with unexpected severity, and she drew in a deep breath trying to control the pain.

"Summer!"

"I'm fine," she said breathlessly.

James pulled into the emergency entrance at Virginia Mason Hospital and raced around the front of the car. He opened the door, unsnapped the seat belt and lovingly helped her out.

Someone rolled a wheelchair toward her, and while Summer sat and answered the questions in Admitting, James parked the car.

She was on the maternity floor when he rejoined her, looking pale and harried.

"Stop worrying," she scolded him.

James dragged a chair to the side of her bed and slumped into it. "Feel my heart," he said and placed her hand over his chest.

"It feels like a machine gun," Summer said, smiling. She moved her hand to his face and cupped his cheek.

"I need you so much," James whispered.

Summer couldn't speak due to a strong contraction. James clasped her hand and talked to her in soothing tones, urging her to relax. As the pain ebbed, she kept her eyes closed.

When she opened them, she found James standing by the hospital bed, studying her. She smiled weakly and he smiled in return.

Dr. Wise arrived and read her chart, then asked, "How are we doing here?"

"Great," Summer assured him.

"Not so good," James said contradicting her. "I think Summer needs something for the pain, and frankly I'm not feeling so well myself."

"James, I'm fine," Summer told him yet again.

"What your husband's saying is that he needs help to deal with seeing you in pain," the physician explained.

"Do something, Doc."

Dr. Wise slapped James affectionately on the back. "Why don't we let Summer be the one to decide if she needs an epidural? She's a better judge than either one of us."

"All right." But James's agreement came reluctantly.

For Summer the hours passed in a blur. Her labor was difficult, and she was sure she could never have endured it if not for James, who stood faithfully at her side. He encouraged her, lifted her spirits, rubbed her back, reassured her of his love.

News of the primary filtered into the room in messages from Charlotte and various nurses, who caught snippets on the waiting room TV. In the beginning Summer strained to hear each bit of information. But as the evening wore on, she became so consumed by what was happening to her and the babies that she barely heard.

She lost track of time, but it seemed to her that it was well into the wee hours of the morning when she was taken into the delivery room.

James briefly left her side and returned a few minutes later, gowned in surgical green. He resembled a prison escapee, and she took one look at him and laughed.

"What's so funny?"

"You."

James drew in a deep breath and held Summer's hand. "It's almost time."

"I know," she breathed softly. "Ready or not, we're about to become parents. I have the feeling this is going to be the ride of a lifetime."

"It's been that way for me from the night I met you."

"Are you sorry, James?"

"Sorry?" he repeated. "No way!" Leaning over, he kissed her forehead. "My only regret is that I didn't marry you that first New Year's."

"Oh, James, I do love you."

Dr. Wise joined them. "Well, you two, let's see what we've got here, shall we?" He grinned at

James. "Congratulations, Your Honor. You won the primary. This is obviously a night for good news."

Two months later Summer woke to the soft, mewling cry of her infant daughter. She climbed silently out of bed and made her way into their daughters' nursery.

There she found James sitting upright in the rocker, sound asleep with Kellie in his arms. Kerrie fussed in her crib.

Lifting the tiny bundle, Summer changed Kerrie's diaper, then sat in the rocker next to her husband and offered the hungry child her breast. Kerrie nursed eagerly and Summer ran her finger down the side of her baby's perfect face.

Her gaze wandered to her husband and she felt a surge of pride and love. The election had been that night, and he'd won the court seat by a wide margin. During the heat of the last two weeks of the campaign, James had let her compose and sing a radio commercial for him. Summer had been proud of her small part in his success, although she didn't miss life on the stage. Her twin daughters kept her far too busy for regrets.

James must have felt her scrutiny because he stirred. He looked up and saw Summer with Kerrie.

"I might as well feed Kellie, too," she said. Experience had taught her that the minute one was fed and asleep, the other would wake and demand to be nursed. Her twin daughters were identical in more than looks. Even their sleep patterns were the same.

James stood and expertly changed Kellie's diaper.

When Kerrie finished nursing, Summer swapped babies with him. James gently placed his daughter on his shoulder and patted her back until they heard the tiny burp.

"Why didn't you wake me?" Summer asked.

"You were sleeping so soundly."

"It was quite a night, Your Honor," she said, looking over at her husband. "I couldn't be more thrilled for you, James. Your position on the bench is secure."

"I couldn't have done it without you," he told her.

"Don't be ridiculous."

"It's true," he said with feeling. "You and Kerrie and Kellie. The voters fell in love with the three of you. Those radio commercials you sang were the talk of the town. I'm the envy of every politician I know."

"Because I can sing?"

"No, because you're my wife." His eyes were dark, intense. "I'm crazy about you, Summer. I still can't believe how much you've given me."

"I love you, too, James." Summer closed her eyes. It had started almost two years ago in Vegas, when it felt as if her heart was breaking. Now her heart was filled to overflowing. Life couldn't get any better than it was right then, she decided.

But Summer was wrong.

Because the best was yet to come.

Center Point Publishing
600 Brooks Road ● PO Box 1
Thorndike ME 04986-0001 USA

(207) 568-3717

US & Canada:
1 800 929-9108
www.centerpointlargeprint.com